Treading the Boards

Celeste Walters

Treading the Boards

LITTLE HARE
www.littleharebooks.com

Little Hare Books
8/21 Mary Street, Surry Hills
NSW 2010 AUSTRALIA

www.littleharebooks.com

First published in 2007

National Library of Australia
Cataloguing-in-Publication entry

Walters, Celeste.
Treading the boards.

For children.
ISBN 978 1 921049 80 4.
ISBN 1 921049 80 4.

1. Children's plays—Juvenile fiction. I. Title.

A823.3

Cover design by Lore Foye
Set in 12/15 pt Bembo by Clinton Ellicott
Printed in Australia by Griffin Press, Adelaide

5 4 3 2 1

For

Guy, Alexander and Alistair

Contents

The Announcement

So here I am, on my way to school on the first day of term, and I ride past Weed's place and give him a yell. Weed is my best buddy. Out he comes and off we sail, yakking as we go. Weed, who is little and weedy, is perched on a big bike, and I, who am tall and unweedy, am nudging the ground on a little one.

We get to school and push into the hall, because on the first day of term there's always assembly. We make straight for the back. I've brought Herb. Herb is my centipede and, sadly, Herb is not fast. Bert, on the other hand, *is* fast. Bert belongs to Zood, who is also my buddy. Zood likes racing centipedes because Bert wins. Bugs is another buddy. He heaves us a wave.

Anyway, here we are at the back of the hall. We've slipped off our chairs onto the floor and our centipedes are lined up and ready to race.

There's silence. Then Mrs Babbage, the principal, starts talking.

Tom (that's me): (whispering) Come on, Herb, you useless dag.

Zood: (whispering) Do you reckon the school would give out an award for racing 'pedes?

Bugs: (whispering) You're pushing Herb. That's cheating.

Zood: (whispering) Where's Bert got to? Ya seen Bert?

Bugs: (whispering) I think I got a 'pede in my sock.

Weed: (whispering) Come on, Bazza! Come on, ya little beauty!

Zood: (looking under the chairs) I can't find Bert. Hey, Bert! Bert!

Weed: (whispering) Come on, Bazza! Good on ya, Bazza. Ya little beauty. Ya little champion.

The voice from the stage says, 'We all know Mr Bloomer's talent for writing, and we're delighted that he has written a play. A play that will involve a whole class.'

Me: What's she saying?

I get up on my knees to see what's going on.

Mrs Babbage: And since Class 8B is Mr Bloomer's class, it seems only fair that they should have the pleasure of putting it on.

Me: (whispering to the guys on the floor) That's us.

Zood: (whispering) Bert! Where's Bert!

Me: (getting to my feet) Hey, that's us—

Zood: (screaming) You dumb jerk! You've squashed Bert!

Bugs: You can have Alf.

Zood: Bert was the best I ever had!

Now assembly is over, and there's pushing and shoving and a grabbing of bags as everyone surges outside. I don't give another thought to what I've heard about the play. At least, not for a few minutes. We're all clumping towards the art room when Weed yells, 'You seen the noticeboard?'

Weed notices what's on noticeboards, and he takes the information fairly seriously.

'It's about this play for term three,' he tells me.

'So?'

'It's term three now. We're the class who are doing it. The audition's today.'

And then, before we know it, it's lunchtime and the whole of Class 8B is assembled back in the hall. Nobody wants to be there, but the notice on the noticeboard states quite clearly that if we don't turn up at lunchtime we'll get a Saturday morning detention.

In comes Sir—that is, Mr Bloomer—and bellows for silence. Then he tells us about his play.

The play is pathetic.

It goes something like this. The wimpish Lady Imogen is abducted from the castle and locked up in a dungeon. After a lot of whingeing and whining, she is rescued by the good knight after he has slain the bad knight and they go off and live happily ever after.

Can you believe it?

Sir, who is now playing big-time-director, is so puffed up about the brilliance of his play that he doesn't seem to notice our groans. Instead, he invites those who want a speaking part in the play to go to the right of the hall, and those who want to be backstage workers, to go to the left.

A sea of bodies stampedes to the left, leaving only five on the right. Jemima, The Brain, Weasel, Jonesey and The Ape. And four of those are only there because they're spaced out about Jemima.

Sir looks dismayed. He claps his hands for silence. 'Let's start again,' he says. 'Everyone spread out around the room.'

Instead of spreading out, bodies duck behind larger bodies.

'That's enough.' Sir points a finger. 'Darius has a strong voice, haven't you, Darius? Your voice is heard all over the playground. Mario, pass him the script. Darius, read from the top of page three.'

Darius (known to us as Weasel): Mmmmmmmmmmmmm.

Sir: I beg your pardon?

Weasel: Mmmmmmmmmmmmmmmmmmmm.

Sir: What was that?

Weasel: (whispering) I'm speaking as loud as I can, Sir. Could I be heard at the back of the hall?

Sir: You'll be perfect for the bad knight. Give Matthew the book.

Matthew: (clutching his neck) I've got a sore throat, Sir.

Sir: Those with sore throats will spend rehearsal time in the sick bay.

Matthew: My throat feels a bit better now, Sir.

Sir: (to Zood) How is the state of your throat, my boy?

Zood: (squeaking) Good, Sir.

This is actually not true. It just so happens that Zood has a very sore throat. But he also has experience of the sick bay and he never wants to go there again.

Zood: (reading) Zis ess er (ah ah) bootifol—

Sir gives Zood the part of a guard.

So far, Weed and I are safe. We're standing behind Mario, who has a very wide back. It's good for hiding behind, and is excellent for racing centipedes on.

Suddenly there is a mighty roar. A centipede has gone down Mario's enormous neck.

'Wonderful!' Sir exclaims. 'Mario, you have the perfect voice for the bad king.'

Mario turns and shoves his face at me. 'I'm gonna kill you,' he hisses.

The audition yawns on like this until Sir has lined up a good knight, a bad knight, a good king, a bad king, a couple of queens, and some random other knights and things, by which time he's looking pretty pleased with himself. The Brain has scored the role of the good knight (who is the prince in disguise) and will play opposite Jemima. This is stiff cheese for Jonesy and The Ape, and it's worse for Weasel, who is the bad knight. You really have to feel a bit sorry for the old Weasel. It's not likely that Lady Imogen would ever go crazy over someone who has to skewer her to the wall five times a week. And that's exactly what it's going to be. Five rehearsals a week, for six weeks. And towards the end, possibly weekends.

Sir is telling us how much fun we're going to have, and how being in a play will teach us to cooperate and pull together. He pauses briefly to stop a fight between Jonesey and The Ape. Then he calls for strong able-bodied types to be the ones who carry bits of furniture about and build the set. All those who haven't yet been given parts start flexing their muscles and barging to the front, we are suddenly very anxious to appear cooperative.

Soon everyone who wants to work behind the scenes has a job. Except for Weed and me, because we are still looking for the centipede that went down Mario's neck. Then Weed is given the job of putting up advertising posters because Mad-Dog, who has been made printer of posters, and Bugs, who is the assistant to the printer of posters, don't also want to be the putters up of posters.

Which leaves me as the only person without a job. I show quick thinking by suggesting that I be assistant curtain puller. And before Sir can say he's never heard of an assistant curtain puller, I point out that Foxy, who is *the* curtain puller, bats for the school cricket team and his hands might get damaged by a cricket ball. If this happened we would need a properly trained replacement curtain puller, for if the curtains slide back at the wrong time, it can be a disaster for everyone.

Rather than waste time arguing, Sir agrees. Though he adds that if anything else comes up, I'll be it.

He hands out sheets of dialogue to the actors.

'Silence!' he calls. He points to Jonesey. 'From the top.'

Jonesey: (adjusting his glasses) He walks quickly towards—

Sir: No, no, no! The first speech.

Jonesey: (again adjusting glasses) I-have-you-in-my-power-you.

Sir: That doesn't sound right.

Jonesey: (peering closely at script) It's a bit of dirt.

Sir: What is a piece of dirt?

Jonesey: Here on the page. I thought it was a full stop.

Sir: (heaving sigh) Try again.

Jonesey: (adjusting glasses) I-have-YOU-in-my-power—

Sir: No, not *you*.

Jonesey: (glasses dropping from nose) What not me?

Sir: It's not, "I have YOU in my power", it's "I have you in my POWER". Hear the difference? Think POWER.

They spend the next twenty minutes sorting that one out, and then Sir turns to the girls.

Sir: Now girls, let's have a bit of sparkle.

Angie: Do I get to keep my costume, Sir?

Sir: We'll all be making our own costumes, Angelica.

Angie: Okay (reading). I can feel the trembling of my poor heart. Oh! It's cracked!

Sir: (studying the page) It doesn't say it's cracked in the script.

Angie: My nail's cracked!

Sir: A cracked nail is nothing to compare with what the good queen, who you are playing, is about to suffer.

Now that the play is cast and the backstage crew appointed, we are dispatched late to various classes where teachers are having a nice yawn and probably thinking that a school play is not such a bad idea after all. Especially if the rehearsals are held frequently and go overtime. I have to agree with them. Assistant curtain puller is hardly stressful. Mad-Dog, Bugs and Weed feel equally cool about their jobs of printer of posters, assistant to the printer of posters and putter up of posters.

Now we can relax and pity those poor dudes who have to learn their scripts off by heart in three weeks.

Being in a play has distinct advantages.

Some
Friend

I'd always thought Zood was my friend. My buddy for life. But you can't trust anyone.

Anyway here we are, the next day, on our way to school. Weed and me on our bikes passing Zood's place and giving him a yell.

Out he comes—and announces that he's off to Greece. They all are—mum, dad, older sister, middle sister, youngest sister, younger brother, baby something and Aunty Voula. Zood's grandma, in Greece, has to have speckles or something dug out of her stomach and they all want to be there to witness it. How grandma ended up with speckles in her stomach is beyond me. Beyond Zood, too. But he's not asking questions. He's going to Greece, sore throat and all.

Well, we congratulate him on all the school he's going to miss out on, and ride away.

The significance of Zood going away doesn't enter my head. In any case, if someone is in your debt, and you remind them of this debt two or three times a day, then you don't expect them to abandon you. Especially not if they want to be a mortician.

It's true. Zood wants to be an undertaker and roll out the stiffs. Roll them out and tuck them up in their little graves. He thinks of nothing else. But to be an undertaker you have to be good at maths. I suppose that's because if you can't measure up the coffins properly, you'll leave the legs sticking out. As it turns out, Zood is *not* good at maths. But I am. And I am also kind-hearted. So guess who's been helping Zood with his homework?

Well, Weed and I ride on saying really nice things about Zood. Which proves that kind-hearted people are right nutters and deserve what they get.

As you are about to see ...

It's two days later, which means it's Friday.

I pull up outside Weed's house on the way to school. He's already outside with his bike and his backpack. And trailing behind is his mum with her bike and her backpack.

Now, Weed's mum is a mother-type version of Weed. Little and weedy with spiked hair, which today is the colour of a ripe nectarine. She waves, and I give her a thumbs up, which means I think she looks cool. Weed's mum is a librarian, and even though I think she looks cool, I'm suspecting that in the public library today there'll be more peering at her hair than peering at books.

She yells goodbye and pedals away.

Weed and I set off for school, jabbering as we go. There are times when I learn a lot from Weed. And today is one of those times. Weed tends to listen at school, while I tend to switch off. Weed says that in English today we are going to learn how to speak. I point out that most of us can do this already, but Weed says we are going to learn to project.

'Project what?' I ask.

But Weed explains that, after hearing this news, he must have switched off too.

We ride on. We pass Zood's place. At this very moment, he's probably on his way to Greece. And not one unkind thought has yet come into my head. In fact, I feel quite envious of Zood's good fortune.

In that positive frame of mind, we get to school.

The first class is English.

Into the classroom steams a female garden gnome of about a hundred and fifty. She's called Mrs Throsby, and she teaches speech.

And she can't pronounce her Rs.

According to Sir, speech training is a must. It will ensure the success of his brilliant play. Though why would it be important for the stage hands, we wonder. Bugs tries to argue this case, only to be told that he needs speech training more than anyone.

According to Mrs Throsby, we must project our voices.

'We must be heard in the back wow,' she gurgles, 'where vewy likely there is someone sitting who we want to impwess.'

I look at Weed. Weed looks at me. This is uncool.

Then we start. First we examine our stomachs for something called a diaphragm.

'To pwoject pwopewly we must bweathe thwough the diaphwagm,' warbles Mrs Throsby.

There's lots of heavy breathing. We stand straight.

Then we exercise the lips, the jaws, the tongue. We make bubble-humming noises, projecting our voices to the ends of our arms, to the far wall, to the hills beyond town. And we are projecting very nicely—so nicely that there's a hefty banging on the wall from the class next door, who are trying to do maths.

'We must pwactise, pwactise, pwactise,' chirrups Mrs Throsby.

We pwactise.

And then our time is up and we stomp out. We make for the science block, bubble humming to the far hills as we go.

The morning sludges on.

Eventually it's lunchtime and here's Weed and Bugs on a bench with their faces in an atlas. Weed is pointing out the places Zood will be flying over on his way to Greece. And I'm trying to work out how much money we will have to save so we can go and visit him. We munch our sandwiches, and again we tell each other how happy we are for Zood, and how we wish him well. Which is something I will not be doing before the end of the day.

Then we make for the hall and the first rehearsal of the play.

Amazingly, for a while everything goes all right. People read their parts, one after the other. Until The Brain, who is the prince in disguise, bawls, '"The moment, at last, is come."'

This is followed by a long silence.

'"The moment, at last, is come!"' he bellows again.

Still nothing.

Sir dives for his script. 'Wake up! Wake up! Guard!'

Silence.

'Guard, say your line!' Sir yells.

But the guard is Zood, and he's not going to wake up and say his line because he's on his way to Greece. And if he is saying anything at all, it is probably in Greek, which isn't going to help the prince.

'Who is the guard?'

'George, Sir. He's gone to Greece, Sir.'

Sir looks stunned at the idea of someone going overseas instead of being in his play. Then his gaze falls on me. I make vigorous curtain-pulling movements. But a gleam has come into Sir's eye.

'You,' he smiles nastily, 'are the guard.'

'But, Sir—'

'Take this script—'

'But—'

'And stand straight. Guards stand straight.'

I hunch on to the stage.

'That slouch is a Saturday-morning-detention body-movement!' he roars.

I convert quickly to a Friday-lunchtime-detention body-movement. I think of Zood. I imagine his legs sticking out of a mahogany casket, his eyeballs staring lifelessly at the nailed-down lid. And this helps me to feel better.

Then I spend the rest of the day trying to swap roles with the backstage crew. I go through everyone. I even promise to do their maths homework for a week. For the term. Forever. But no go.

You just can't rely on anyone.
There is nothing in life to be pleased about.
Except that I squashed Bert.

On the Home Front

My mother's a born actress. It's sad to think her career stopped when she was thirteen, because she would have smashed the box office. As it is, now she just smashes objects—such as bone china—when she's being dramatic. In fact, during one spectacular display of bad temper on her last birthday, she sent Dad fleeing to a flat on the thirty-sixth floor of an apartment block in the city.

He still comes over regularly, usually just before dinner; or when there's some arty movie that Mum *has* to see and she wants someone to go with her.

It's weird.

People say, 'Your mum and dad together?'

'Nah.'

'Divorced?'

'Nah.'

'Separated?'

'Nah.'

Also, they talk to each other on the phone at least once a day. Sometimes more. It usually ends with her sending something flying against the wall. But, more often than not, half an hour later, she's dialling his number again.

I tell you, it's weird. When Arabella Philpott broke my heart in kindergarten because she wouldn't share her jelly beans, I never spoke to her again.

Of course, it could be worse. At least Dad lives in his flat by himself. Mad-Dog's dad lives in *his* flat with a Hollywood-type blonde. Mad-Dog is not happy about this. Neither is his mum.

Bugs says that parents who laugh together, stay together. And he should know because both his parents are dentists and dentists have always got something to laugh about. However, the slightest hint of a giggle from one of *my* parents tends to provoke a major meltdown in the other. The only likelihood of them ever laughing together is if one of them fell off a ladder watching the other break a leg on a banana skin.

Anyway, my problem, with Dad gone, is that all Mum's heavy dramatics are launched at me. So, you can imagine her reaction when I drag myself in from school and tell her about my speaking role in the play.

What I actually want from her is sympathy. I want pity. I want my mum to say, 'There, there, we'll make the horrible thing go away.' It worked like a dream when I was little. She fixed everything from sprained ankles to Arabella Philpott.

But not today.

Instead she is overjoyed. 'My boy is treading the boards!' she gushes, and throws her arms around me. She could simply have said, 'He's in a play.' But you don't know my mum.

Then she immediately rings Dad. 'Thomas is strutting the stage,' she announces. 'He takes after us ... What? No, not your family. *My* family. The artistic side.'

I have to listen to all this.

Then she decides she's going to celebrate. She invites Dad to join our Sunday roast. Grandma gets an invite, too.

Grandma's pretty groovy, even if she is a bit deaf and large. Well, large for a grandma. When she laughs her chins wobble. Her boobs, too. Big boobs that are nice to cuddle into when you're little and have hurt your knee. And, if you can steer her away from how you're doing at school, she's good for a laugh. As well as for a bit of ready cash.

Gloop, of course, will be there as well.

It's hard to describe Gloop. He's not your ordinary dog, though he does ordinary dog-type things and eats ordinary dog-type food and barks an ordinary dog-type bark. Gloop's different because he looks sad. All the time. You've never seen a dog look so sad. Even when he's happy, which is most of the time, he looks sad. His face is the problem, and his ears. His face is long and his ears are long and they both droop and his eyes sort of droop too. It's pretty dumb when you're happily leaping around with your tail wagging madly to have such a sad expression. But that's Gloop. You mightn't think he's smart, but he is. And he's a great fighter. It's just that his looks can put you off a bit.

So that's Grandma and Gloop.

And now you'll meet Dad, too, because today it's Sunday.

I'm putting the knives and forks on to the table. Gloop's wagging his tail and looking sad at the prospect of a meaty bone, Grandma is yakking on to Dad and Dad has his head in a newspaper.

Now, my dad is not a little man, even if he has only a little hair. My dad is big, like Grandma. He would make a cool guard because he stands very straight, which is amazing considering the amount of stuff that's been thrown at him. He's also one of those boring, successful types. My dad's a barrister. People pay heaps for Dad just to listen to them. Which he isn't doing now, even though Grandma's yakking at him.

Suddenly his head appears. He eyeballs me. 'What's another word for *attack* in seven letters?'

'I dunno.'

'Starts with A.'

'Army?'

Dad sighs. 'Here's an easier one. *Agree* in six letters.'

'Um . . .'

'Starts with C.'

'C?'

'Concur,' my mother hisses as she whips past.

'Education today is a joke,' says my father to the newspaper. 'Kids can't read, they can't spell, they've got to have machines to add up—'

'Welcome to the visual world,' chimes my mother, stirring gravy.

'I was reading Dickens and Conrad at his age.'

'Mum's right,' I say, speaking to the head that's now back behind the newspaper. 'There's this program on the telly about endangered species. Everybody sees it except me.'

'I love that program, too, Pet,' pipes up Grandma.

'I love those little creatures with the waggly tails that squeak—'

'And we're talking about the program in class,' I continue, still talking to the newspaper. 'And since I'm the only one in the class who hasn't seen it, my marks will most likely be very low ...'

The head reappears, and eyes focus on me. 'There are books, you know. Libraries are full of them. And when you pick up a book, not only are you learning about the subject in hand—which can include endangered species—but, importantly, you will be learning how the English language works ... Are you listening to me?'

'Yeah.'

'You're a lucky boy, Tom,' says Dad. 'You've inherited the language of Shakespeare and Milton.'

Fortunately dinner is now on the table, with steam rising from the potatoes and pumpkin, and a delicious aroma rising from the sliced leg of lamb.

I shoot Gloop a look which warns him to be ready, if necessary, to beat a hasty retreat. Because the table conversation, which is supposed to focus on my part in the play, starts like this:

Grandma: Myrtle's not well.

Mum: Oh?

Dad: Where's the mint sauce?

Mum: There's no mint sauce. There's no mint.

Grandma: Not a bit well.

Dad: There's truck-loads of mint down the side of the house.

Mum: Then you pick it.

Grandma: It's her bowels.

Mum: And you make it.

Dad puts his plate on top of the oven and goes outside.

Mum: Good!

Grandma: Oh no, it's not good. A healthy bowel means a healthy body. Tom's a healthy boy, aren't you, Pet? Now, what is he up to at school?

Mum: I told you, Daphne. He's got an important role in the school play. Tom has artistic talent.

Grandma: I was in a play when I was at school . . .

Dad re-enters with a fistful of mint.

Grandma: I was a fairy.

And she's telling us all about it.

Dad is at the sink with vinegar and boiling water.

Dad: Now my dinner'll be cold.

Mum: Well it was you who wanted mint sauce.

Next thing there's roaring and yelling because Dad's cut his finger chopping mint and mum's shouting that it wasn't her who turned the oven off, it's the wonky thermostat, and Gran's going on about fairies and how sensitive to people's feelings they are, and how the world would be better off if we were more like them. And Gloop's under the table.

Me: Gotta go. Rehearsal.

Which isn't strictly the case, but you don't want to hear any more, do you?

More on the Home Front

Today is my birthday.

It starts with a kiss from my mother and, 'Something's on the kitchen table.'

Which sounds promising.

Mum knows what I want. Dad knows what I want. Gran knows what I want. Gloop knows what I want. The whole world knows what I want. I want a TV.

I zoom to the kitchen, and I must admit the square box does look promising, towering, as it does, above the orange juice and the cornflakes.

I suppose you've already guessed the sad truth. I live in a television-free zone.

On this matter, Mum and Dad are as one. Both are readers. Books clog every mantelpiece and spare flat surface. Books languish in bedrooms, by bathtubs; they stand like security guards on either side of the loo in case you get bored.

Weed and the others call me a deprived child, which expresses the situation very nicely as I am deprived of perhaps the most important thing in life. But I do have buddies. Good buddies. Buddies whose mums don't mind if people come and watch telly in their houses. Though it's not a lot of fun to be at your buddy's place when the phone rings and you're told that your mum wants you home in two minutes. Which always seems to happen just as some starship is about to be attacked.

Nevertheless, the box rising from the table does look promising.

I rip at the wrapping paper, claw at the cardboard, and feel something hard and smooth.

'It's something you'll really love,' says Mum.

Goody, goody, goody.

'Something you'll always have.'

I stare at what's been unwrapped. I stare at Gloop. Gloop stares back.

I've unwrapped what seems to be a model of an android spacecraft. No, that's not what it is. It's the model of some sort of theatre. My mother flicks a switch and the model stage floods with light.

'It's The Globe!' she squeals. 'Shakespeare's theatre, built in 1614.'

Gloop sludges off under the table. He always responds with great sympathy to my pain. He also senses when it's going to get worse. Which he seems to be sensing now.

And he's right. The phone goes.

'Happy birthday, Pet.'

'Ta, Gran.'

'And what did you get?'

'Mum already told you, I bet.'

'She did,' says Gran. 'She was so excited. And I've got

you something to go with it. I found a lovely copy in a shop in the arcade ...'

'Ta, Gran ...'

Meanwhile, Mum has loaded other parcels onto the table. 'From your father,' she explains.

'I thought we were all going to dinner tonight?'

'We are. But he wanted you to get them first thing, so he left them here yesterday.'

I stare at the two parcels, one square, one flat.

'Aren't you going to open them?'

I open the flat one first. It's a jacket, a blazer type thing with gold buttons. The sort that old sailors wear when they're laid out in armchairs waiting to die. The second is a book. It's called *Fowler's Modern English Usage*.

'You are truly deprived,' says Weed. Weed could almost be described as intellectual when he's in a thoughtful mode. 'Truly deprived. And on your birthday that's sad.'

I don't reply, because sad is precisely what I am. We ride towards school in silence.

We are running very late. Classes may already have begun. But because of my birthday, and being deprived, and telling Weed all about it, we are now what you might call 'wagging it'.

Suddenly Weed stops. He's had an idea. And the idea is so excellent that he falls off his bike and uses bad language. Which is not very pleasant for someone to hear on their birthday. But, you see, Weed has been thinking laterally. And when you think laterally you see things differently and use language more imaginatively than usual.

But as it happens—though he doesn't know it, and though he's trying to cheer me up—the result of Weed's lateral thinking will soon heave my birthday, and me with it, into a very different reality zone.

So here's Weed sitting in the gutter, fishing into his pocket and pulling out a crumpled twenty dollar note.

'What's that for?' I ask.

'Chops and stuff. For dinner. I've got to buy it after school. But we won't be having chops and stuff for dinner. Not tonight we won't.'

'Why not?'

'Because I've lost my twenty bucks.'

'Your twenty bucks is right there,' I say, pointing. The thing is clutched in his grimy paw.

Weed grins. 'It won't be. Not after we've relieved the corner shop of a couple of smoothies, some two-layer double-cream chocolate cakes and that—'

'What about school?'

'I'll say you puked up and I had to take you home.' Weed pauses, again thinking laterally. 'Which will probably be true.'

I'm thinking that being in our school uniforms is not a good idea, particularly when people in school uniform are supposed to be in class by now, not in coffee shops.

Still, it's my birthday.

We approach the trendy little cafe with its striped awnings and small round tables, leave our bikes outside and angle our way through the coffee sippers to the counter, where the cakes are displayed in glass cabinets.

While Weed orders the smoothies, I study the cakes.

Cakes with layers of cream and strawberries. Cakes with chocolate piled on top. Banana cakes shaped like boats made with real banana. Cakes topped with meringue and blueberries. Big cakes, little cakes of a million mouth-watering colours and shapes.

'Wow,' gurgles Weed, pointing at an enormous cherry-tipped number, 'grab an eyeful of that one!'

I don't reply.

I've been peering around for a table for two and have grabbed an eyeful of something completely else. And, as a result of this eyeful, I can't speak, let alone move.

And now Weed has seen a spare table and is beckoning me with his head, as his hands are carrying two smoothies. But I just stand there, seeing what I'm seeing.

Weed turns and sees it too. We stare at what we're seeing. Then we stare at each other. And then at them again. At my father and another female person who is most definitely not my mother. But a person whose hand Dad is holding in a not-at-all business-like or fatherly fashion.

Weed lunges back to the counter, pays and squeaks strange apologetic sounds at the lady at the till. Smoothies shudder and spill.

'Move!' he hisses to me.

We both scramble for the door and, in doing so, Weed knocks over a chair which collides with a high chair, which collides with a waitress carrying a tray.

Under cover of chaos and noise we land in the street.

'Well, pluck a duck,' declares Weed.

We haul our bikes onto the road.

'Well, pluck a duck,' he repeats. 'And on your birthday.'

We wobble on.

I'm not going to tell you how I'm feeling. That's my business. But I will say this: I am going to be doing a lot of thinking that will not necessarily be lateral.

But first, there's tonight. My birthday dinner.

Still More on the Home Front

It is 7.15. Mum and I are sitting at a table in an Indian restaurant because Mum likes Indian food. Even though it's *my* birthday. The third chair at the table is for my dad. And it's empty because he's not there.

Twenty minutes later, in he charges.

Mum: (scowling) You're late.

Dad: (huffing and puffing) Had to get a proposal out.

I don't want to look at him. I don't look at him. He thinks he's so big-time he can do anything, get away with anything. I won't talk to him. Let him suffer . . .

The conversation begins and goes something like this:

Dad: Happy birthday, Tom.

I won't talk to him.

I get a whack on the shin from Mum's shoe.

Me: (not looking at him) I got the present.

Dad: Will it fit?

I think to myself, yeah, an old geezer of about a hundred and fifty.

Mum: (to him) Before I forget, put the twenty-sixth in your diary.

Dad: What's on the twenty-sixth?

Mum: The play.

Dad: What play?

Mum: *Tom's* play.

Dad: (flicking through his diary) The twenty-sixth could be difficult.

Mum: It most certainly will be for you if you're not there.

Dad: (to me, with an uncertain look) Into theatre, eh?

Me: You don't *have* to come. Unless, of course you want to bring someone.

Dad: (tucking into the red wine) Who would I bring?

Me: Anyone you might want to take out—like for a coffee or something . . .

Dad: (looking around) Service is slow here.

Me: It's not slow at that other joint.

Mum: What other joint?

Me: The one at the end of Risley Street.

Mum: That's only for coffee and cake.

Me: (to the ceiling) And for people who don't want to be seen.

Dad: You can't *not* be seen there. That place is always crammed to the rafters.

Me: Like my school hall will be on the night of my play, so you can put your diary away.

Dad: I can't be sure what I'll be doing, that's all.

Mum: Now you've hurt his feelings. And on his birthday, too.

Dad: I didn't mean that. You know what I mean, Tom.

Me: (silently inside my head) Yeah, I know exactly what you mean and what you're up to.

Dad: Where for God's sake is the waiter? Waiter!

Mum: Keep your voice down. You're not in court now, showing off.

Dad: Showing off, as you put it, provides you with a nice little income—free of tax.

Mum: I work! You don't think I could survive on . . .

I leave them to it and head for the loo.

I sit on the lavatory seat, staring at the tiles on the floor. The seat is cool. I just might stay here forever. Day by day, year by year becoming more ossified, cemented by bone to the lavatory seat.

I try to think laterally.

Tiles equals bathroom, equals building, equals floors of building, equals thirty-sixth floor of building, equals apartments on thirty-sixth floor of building . . . and apartments equals visitors. Visitors who are blonde, who like to drink coffee and eat cake and have their hands held.

I stop. I consider. I leap.

What could be more logical, more lateral? More simple?

I know what I'll do. I'll turn up at Dad's apartment. I'm his son. What could be more natural? I'll turn up at odd times, when he's likely to be hanging around. And though he'll ask me to tell him next time when I'm coming, I won't. I'll just turn up again, say I'm sorry, I forgot. Or something.

What I'll do when I find them together, I don't know. I'll work that out when I get to it.

And Weed'll come with me.

I return to the table in a brighter birthday mood.

My plan is fail-proof.

Painting the Set

It is a school day. At first I'm not sure which school day. Since my birthday, which was a long time ago, like two days, I have had other things on my mind. I'm not concentrating. I forget things. I front up to the wrong classes. Go to the wrong classrooms. Can't remember where I put things. Forget my lunch.

Weed has been thinking laterally for me because my plan, he reckons, has a serious flaw. But he has failed to come up with an alternative. My plan means getting up early. On a Saturday or a Sunday. I point out that Saturday and Sunday mornings are probably the only times you'd find a barrister at home.

I also point out that, on weekends, barristers who live on a thirty-sixth floor will probably indulge in a slap-up breakfast. I say this because I know that Weed is sick of his mum's organic muesli. Every morning he tells me so. He also tells me that he likes the idea of seeing the world from a thirty-sixth floor . . .

And now I see paint pots lined up along the wall in the school hall and I remember that on Wednesday we are painting the set for the moronic play because the guys who've been slaving away in woodwork to build it have announced that the set is finished. Almost.

And it's Wednesday lunchtime and we're all gathered together being heavily cooperative. We're being heavily cooperative because nobody wants a Saturday morning detention. There are some who are being more cooperative than others. Like The Brain and Jemima, who spend endless hours behind the shelter sheds, cooperatively rehearsing their lines.

Speaking of lines, my one line isn't the breakdown material I thought it would be. It is, after all, only four little words.

Sir strides in and tells us to carry the paint pots to the stage. Then he makes the mistake of asking each of us what we would like to paint. Everybody stampedes towards the drawbridge. And a couple of buckets of grey paint spill and stream on to the floor of the hall.

Sir tries again. He appoints me as backdrop man, which isn't too bad as there are some rather cool turrets and a long covered walkway over which good knights can throw their spears. He also appoints Weed, Jonesey and The Ape to help me.

We contemplate the enormous stretch of cloth laid out on the floor. It is cut into two six-metre lengths. Armed with cardboard templates of turret-shapes and covered ways, and with buckets of grey and black paint, we split up into two groups, drop to the floor and begin.

I have to admit that it isn't as boring as I'd expected. It's actually rather excellent. The paint is sloshable, and it's satisfying to see how easily it can be flicked from the brush onto a passing nerd.

I look around. Before my very eyes there is an example of one-hundred-percent cooperation. Everybody is looking very happy spreading paint everywhere, and since our uniform is grey, they are probably being a bit more experimental than they need to be. Over in the corner, Nigel is working away on the hanging screen which the bad knights will hide behind for spying. Nigel is going to be a big-time artist, a fact that he advertises loudly and so often that he gets to use most of the coloured paint.

In the centre, Mad-Dog is keen to see a beautiful drawbridge, and he's slapping on paint before he's even tried the thing out. Angie and her mob are upside down in the moat. Bugs and company are slapping gold over bits of cardboard for the throne. And another lot are painting the portcullis— which, for those who were not born in the Middle Ages, is a grating over gateways that slides up and down, through which inside dudes can size up outside dudes and decide whether or not to let them in.

Despite Nigel's colours and Bugs's gold, everything in the hall, whether it's supposed to or not, is starting to turn a nice shade of grey.

And then, suddenly, it's time to finish and we're amazed because it seems that we have been painting in the hall for only a few minutes. Which proves how time flies when you're being cooperative.

Sir praises us all and then examines our handiwork.

He starts with my team. He looks at the two lengths of grey, black-edged turrets and the covered walkways and beams. Then he suggests that we put the two lengths together and hang them up to get the finished effect. This is a mistake. One of the lengths has been painted upside down, which means that one half of the turrets are about four metres higher than the others. Which means that anyone wanting to stroll along a covered walkway will have to take a four-metre leap to get from one turret to the next. Sir turns a little pale.

Nigel interrupts the contemplation of this problem to announce that, because he is so talented, he has painted not one spy screen, but two. For the time being, no one takes any notice of this piece of information, including Sir. But later, they realise that they should have.

'Courage,' says Sir, and points to the throne.

We gather around the gold-painted, jewel-encrusted cardboard. Sir's smile, now broad again, pauses mid-beam. 'What is this?' he asks. There are words painted in black letters on the back of the throne: *Requiescat in Pace*.

'That means Rest in Peace,' shrieks Sir. 'You put that on gravestones when people die.'

Sir has gone pale again, and has a look about him that suggests he might be very close to Resting in Peace himself.

Then someone on the other side of the hall bellows, 'Hey, Sir, come and look at Mad-Dog's drawbridge.'

We heave to the right. We watch as the grey-painted drawbridge creaks up, stops, then creaks down again. It's a brilliant feat of engineering. Everybody applauds wildly. Mad-Dog's fangs can be seen in the shape of a grin. The rest of him, that hasn't been painted grey, is black with sump oil from the heavy chain that he's flogged from the trucking company where his dad works.

There are so many shouts of appreciation for Mad-Dog and the trucking company that Mad-Dog starts to show off.

'It'll hold anyone,' he crows. 'Who wants to have a go?'

Silence.

'Where's Weed?'

'I don't think—' says Sir, but his voice is lost in the crowd that surges forward.

And there's Weed on the drawbridge and up he goes. Up, up, up. And there he stays, waving madly. Below, the crowd goes ape with appreciation.

'Stop!' Sir screams. 'Bring him down!'

But the greasy chain has snapped (which doesn't say much for the trucking company). And now Weed is wedged between the top of the drawbridge and the ceiling. It looks as though he is bound to stay there for quite some time. But he doesn't seem to mind. He just waves his arms around a bit and yells that he can see some coral and a very pretty starfish in the moat.

'You can't have starfish in a moat!' Sir wails.

But Angie and her mob can. Also crabs, and conch-shells, and oysters opening up to show off their little pearls, and seahorses and lobsters. And a few hammerhead sharks.

Sir doesn't say much more. But he does stagger a bit as he moves off in the direction of the portcullis whose vertical bars show a distinct lean to the left.

'Perhaps we could stand it on its side, Sir,' suggests some genius.

'*Our* bars are straight, Sir,' chorus a group of window-painters, holding up their windows.

'So are ours,' chorus another lot, holding up theirs.

As it happens, these two groups are sworn enemies and don't communicate. The result is that half the windows have vertical bars and the other half have bars that are horizontal.

This is too much for Sir. The big-time-director is approaching meltdown. He's a funny colour. He points a trembling finger at Weed. 'G-g-get that boy down.'

But how?

There's a chorus of suggestions. A racing for the telephone in the foyer.

And soon Weed, who, from his position on the ceiling can see into the street, squeals, 'The fire brigade!'

Men in yellow helmets storm in.

Sir wobbles to his feet. 'We've got a boy,' he stutters. 'Stuck to the ceiling.'

Funny Business

'We've gotta snoop around,' I say. 'We've gotta watch him, see how he freaks out when the phone rings.'

'Find evidence,' adds Weed. 'Lipstick on a glass, a little lace hanky. That sort of thing.'

'We've gotta act casual, too. We have to say stuff like, "we were just passing".'

'At seven in the morning?'

'Or we could give some reason why we couldn't sleep.'

'That's true,' says Weed, and stifles a yawn.

It's Saturday morning. We're heading for my father's apartment and have stopped at a newspaper stall for a packet of chips.

'What if we find him on the balcony sipping orange juice with someone, who just may be a blonde someone?' I ask. 'What then?'

'We tell her who we are, and we ask your dad who she is, and why she is there. And then we wait.'

We finally arrive.

The lift is express to the thirty-sixth floor.

'Wow,' ogles Weed.

We edge along caramel carpet flanked by floor-to-ceiling glass. Past urns of feathery fronds. Past wall sculptures of fawns frisking in Arcadian fields.

We get to number seventeen. I knock.

There is a pause. It's a long enough pause for someone to shove an embarrassing guest into a cupboard.

Then the door opens.

'Hello,' Dad says, looking surprised. He's wearing casual trousers and a gold shirt with the sleeves rolled up.

I nudge Weed forward. 'He's hungry,' I say. 'Me too.'

'I'm just about to leave,' Dad says. 'I have to meet a client. But there's muesli in the cupboard.'

Weed shoots me a dirty look.

'Weed's studying views,' I say. 'I told him about the view from here.'

Dad lets us in and gestures vaguely toward the windows.

'Wow!' gasps Weed again. 'Wow!'

The view really is something. On one side rises the city, through which the river flows like a grey ribbon. And stretching beyond, as far as the hills, are rows and rows of matchbox suburbs. On the other side of the apartment, if you look down, there are the railway yards with model trains shunting to and fro. If you look up, you see the sea.

Everything inside the apartment is high-tech. Mostly steel. Including the fridge.

'Clients on a Saturday,' I say.

'Often on a Sunday as well,' says Dad, who has disappeared into the bathroom.

I yank Weed away from the window. 'Quick! Search!'

I fling open cupboards, flick eyes into drawers, across pillows, under beds. I check out the laundry.

'Can't find any lipstick traces,' hisses Weed from the kitchen.

'There's no little hanky hanging around either,' I hiss back. 'She's quick.'

'Who's your client?' I call.

'No one you'd be interested in.'

Dad reappears, smelling of aftershave. Weed and I exchange looks. He knows that I know that when people try to smell nice, it's most likely because they want to impress someone. Such as a blonde.

He tells us to clean up and lock up after ourselves.

Then the doorbell goes again. It's Grandma, clutching a green bag.

In she sails. 'I want to talk to you,' she says, fixing her eyes on Dad's trousers and gold shirt.

Dad grabs his briefcase. 'I'm late for breakfast with a client.'

'I'm having problems with the council—'

'Make an appointment like everybody else.' As Dad starts towards the door, the phone on the kitchen bar rings. He doubles back and snatches up the receiver. 'Yes?'

Grandma plonks down her bag. 'Hello, Pet, what are you doing here?' She gives me a kiss and looks at Weed. 'Who are you?'

'This is Weed, Gran.'

'Are you in Tom's class, Reed?'

'Yeah.'

'Do you read, Reed?'

'Weed's the biggest reader in the class. The best listener, too.'

Grandma beams. 'Excellent. Tom needs a good friend. Do you have a grandmother, Reed?'

'Yeah, two.'

'Poor boy. Then I can be your grandmother. Write down your birthday, Reed, and I shall send you a card.'

Weed shoots me a puzzled look.

Angry expressions and very rude words are coming from the kitchen. We try to listen.

Grandma continues. 'And you have a mother and a father, Reed?'

'No, um . . .'

This is true. Sad, too. Weed's dad was under the Dog's Head Bridge when it toppled (so much for wearing a helmet). But he does have a mum.

Now there's the sound of a phone being slammed down, and Dad, very red in the face, storms from the kitchen.

'I won't stand for it!' he roars.

'Nor me,' adds Grandma. 'It's the community bus. The council's intending to change the route—'

Dad is stuffing things into a briefcase and muttering through clenched teeth. 'She can find someone else. I simply won't stand for it.'

This sounds good. This sounds like the blonde has let him down. And that it's over.

'So you're not going to breakfast after all?' I ask.

Grandma smiles. 'He's going to help me instead.'

'I am not going to help you. I am going to breakfast. Where are my keys?'

I hiss at Grandma. 'Who's he going to meet?'

Grandma glares at her son. 'Who *are* you going to meet? Who is more important than me? I need advice. I made you a cake.'

'Who I go to breakfast with is my affair,' snarls Dad. 'I am late and I am leaving now.'

With that, my father, his briefcase and his keys are gone.

Grandma turns to me. 'Funny business,' she remarks. 'Oh well!' She dives into her green bag and pulls out a strawberry layer cake. 'Put the kettle on, Reed. It's time for morning tea.'

Weed obliges.

Later Weed tells me that while the next plan will have to be somewhat more fail-proof, he has had an excellent morning. He also says that though Gran mightn't be all there in the hearing department, she's still pretty groovy. And a grandma who serves strawberry layer cake for break-fast is a grandma worth treasuring.

Fire and
Passion

It is Monday. We've already had two weeks of rehearsals, and I'm thinking that being in a play can be quite a positive experience. Particularly when you get to miss half your maths classes and all of Indonesian.

I'm also considering the next move I will make on *him*. I've been thinking about this all weekend. I know one thing. I'm going to confide in Gran.

Gran's large. She's loud. She would scare the pants off anyone when she's mad. Maybe, just maybe, I can leave the whole thing to her.

I'm starting to feel better.

I must get back to concentrating.

And today the sun is shining, the birds are chirping and I'm wheeling slowly home from school with Weed and Bugs. We pass by a tree under which The Brain and Jemima are rehearsing their lines. We whistle and yell a few rude words.

They wave and keep at it.

I'm thinking that if I didn't have big-time personal concerns on the home front, life would be good.

But I do have big-time personal concerns.

Weed and I are revealing some of the details of the coffee-shop experience to Bugs.

Bugs says, 'Well, pluck a duck. And on your birthday.'

Weed, who has been silent and thinking laterally, says, 'You've just gotta face him about it.'

'Yeah,' agrees Bugs. Then adds, 'How?'

'You've gotta go up to him and say, "I saw you in the coffee shop with that blonde lady."'

We wheel on.

'But,' Weed says, 'there could be a problem.'

'What sort of problem?'

'He's a barrister. And barristers are slick with things like words, and at quoting from books and flinging their arms around.' Weed pauses. 'It's all right if you have a heap of cash and can get a barrister of your own to do the talking for you, but if you can't afford one you can forget it.'

I don't know what Weed is going on about, unless he's remembering the time when people were trying to get compensation from the company that built the shonky bridge that fell on his dad. 'You've gotta watch lawyers, is all I'm saying.'

I'm still not exactly sure what I've got to watch, so I say, 'He's always coming round for dinner.'

'So, nail him when he comes around.'

'Nail him,' echoes Bugs.

'But,' says Weed, 'he might just say, "You're wrong. Never been in the joint." Or, "Well, it's a nice place, good coffee."' Weed pauses. 'Then will come the punchline. "Why didn't you come over and say hello," he'll ask, "and then you could have told us why you and your friend were not at school." With the Law, you always gotta be careful.'

I'm about to remind Weed that it's my dad he's talking about. Then I realise Weed's only trying to help. And then I'm thankful that it wasn't my dad who was defending the company that his dad worked for. Because then me and Weed mightn't have been buddies at all.

We've reached Weed's house and I am taking off to the right and Bugs is going off to the left. We wave rude gestures as we go.

'I've just got in,' a voice shrieks as I go in the front door. I dump my bag and clomp upstairs.

My mother is in her bedroom. 'It took me twenty minutes to find a parking spot today. Twenty minutes! I'd be better off taking the bus. But why should I? Why should I? And if they think that I'm going to pay for a car park when I'm only working part-time, then they're wrong. My front tooth looks discoloured. Don't you think it looks discoloured? It looks discoloured to me.'

I study my mother as she studies her tooth in the mirror. Fortunately her welcome-home speech does not require an answer. No one can answer their own questions in as much detail as my mother. She's on the school committee and it makes you wonder if anyone else gets a word in.

As I head for the stairs, I see the Volvo pull in to the driveway. My father drives a specially imported Volvo. It's silver with leather seats.

I hate it.

So, he's coming for dinner. He cancelled on Sunday.

When I tried to find out why, it was the same story: he was working.

I don't want to see him.

I make for the kitchen, raid the fridge, slink about in the sunroom, hear my mother come downstairs, the front door open.

'I'm here,' he calls.

He'll be in the lounge room, reading. As always.

My mother's in the kitchen putting something on the stove. Now she's found me lurking in the sunroom. 'Well?' she says.

'Well what?'

'How did it go?'

'How did what go?'

She gives me an incredulous look. 'The rehearsal.'

'Okay.'

'I still haven't heard your lines.'

She hasn't heard my lines because, as you know, there's only one. And only a four-word line, at that.

'It's in the blood,' she says. 'And from this you'll move on to the great parts. Hamlet, Lear, Othello. But let me hear your lines.'

'I've only got one.'

'Oh.'

It's such a tragic 'Oh' that I say, 'It's a very important line. The whole play hinges on it.'

'It does?' My mother clutches at this promise like a drowning man clutches a branch.

'You see,' I go on, 'the prince, who's disguised as the good knight, finally escapes from the bad knight and his demon henchmen, and returns to the castle. But before he can rescue the Lady Imogen, who's in exile, he's got to prove that he really is the prince. That's when I say my line.'

'Well, say it.'

'"Reveal yourself and flee." I'm the guard.'

'Good. Try it again. This time with more vigour.'

'"Reveal yourself and flee."'

'I can see we will have to work on this.'

For one line!

This is too much. 'Something's boiling!' I yell.

My mother runs to the kitchen.

I get up. As I expected, my father's in the lounge room. He's reading some notes.

I hear Weed's voice in my head, telling me to 'Just do it.'

'Hi,' I say.

Eyes appear above the papers. 'Hello.' They disappear again.

'I saw you,' I say. 'I saw you the other day ... week. At that coffee joint at the end of Risley Street.'

'Great little cafe.'

'You were with someone.'

'Why didn't you come over and say hello?'

He is answering and reading at the same time.

I say, 'Did you make the breakfast on Saturday?'

'Yes.'

'I was worried about that person on the phone that you had to get rid of. Did she find someone else?'

'She did.'

'Isn't that a bit sad?'

My father suddenly puts down what he's reading and

looks at me. He has eyes that pierce through you. He's got that down to a fine art. 'I suggest that you let me know when you're coming to the apartment in future,' he says.

'Why?'

'It could be awkward.'

'I don't mind waiting.'

'If you've got time to spend your day waiting around, you obviously haven't got enough to do.' Eyes go back to the notes.

My mother comes in right on cue. 'I've just been hearing Tom's line,' she says. 'For the play.'

'Oh.'

She whisks the papers out of Dad's hands. 'It's a very important line. The whole play hinges on it. Let's hear you, Tom.'

' "Reveal yourself and flee." '

'No, no, no! "And FLEEE." More feeling, more fire, more passion.'

' "Relieve yourself and FLEEEEEEEEEE." '

'No. That was wrong.'

'I said, "Reveal yourself and flee." '

'No, you didn't. Not the second time. You said, "Relieve yourself and flee." And that's altogether different. And not very appropriate. Try again.'

Well, this is the start of the nightmare. A terrible, continuing nightmare that haunts my days, and then haunts my nights from the moment I fall asleep. A nightmare in which a huge head—hairless, mouthless and noseless—looms closer and closer, until *snap!* one eye opens and screams *'Reveal'*, and *snap!* the other eye opens and screams *'Relieve'*.

They keep snapping open and closed, open and closed: '*Reveal, relieve, reveal, relieve, reveal, relieve.*'

First my father, now this. I think I am approaching brain overload. By opening night I'll be a wreck.

'It's just as well I'm here to coach you,' my mother declares.

I have to agree. After all, as she says, this line is no ordinary line. The whole play hinges on it.

I'm starting to believe this myself.

'*Reveal, reveal, reveal . . .*'

Miss J Effington-Smythe

It's the following day. It's lunchtime and I'm heading for the hall because it's rehearsal time. I'm walking slowly. The play is in the third week of rehearsals and I am in the first week of a monumental double-header personal meltdown.

An ice-cream in a flabby cone on a 45-degree day. That's me.

I sludge on.

However, it soon dawns on me that I'm the only one walking slowly towards the hall. In fact, I am the only one heading that way at all. I must have missed out on some vital information. Where's Weed when you need him?

But everyone is already *in* the hall. The seats have been stacked at the sides, and people are standing about smiling and nodding and whispering and being very well-behaved and professional indeed.

And then I see why.

She is standing in front of the stage with Sir. And she is blonde, blue-eyed and a smasher.

Sir tells us her name. It is Miss J Effington-Smythe. She smiles. There is silence, because for the first time in Sir's teaching career, everyone wants to listen to what he has to say next.

Sir explains that Miss J Effington-Smythe is a lecturer in drama at some university and, being a friend of Sir (this sounds more hopeful than likely), she has come to give us the benefit of her expertise. Which we are going to fully appreciate.

Oh yes, Sir, we are. Already the play is appearing less moronic and people are pulling out their diaries to make sure that every rehearsal date is underlined in red. Because here is Hollywood standing right in front of us in the exquisite form of Miss J Effington-Smythe.

'Good afternoon, everyone.' She smiles again. When most people smile they just screw up their nose and expose a row of ugly white planks, but not Miss J Effington-Smythe. When she smiles, her eyes shine like stars, her teeth sparkle like diamonds and two little dimples dance, like butterflies, on her cheeks. And as she smiles, her blue eyes dart around the room and catch mine. I know she smiles right at me. I just know she does.

Oh, Miss J Effington-Smythe, you are the most beautiful, the most exquisite, the most heavenly, the most adorable, the most perfect creature in the whole world. If only I could demonstrate to you my slave-like devotion . . .

Suddenly she turns, tiny gold curls dancing, and her flower-like skirt knocks a script off the table. I charge forward, together with Jonesey, who loses his glasses. And I get there first. The script is in my grimy fist. Suddenly I am embarrassed about the state of my fingernails. And this is very strange.

'What's your name?' she asks.

'Tom ... er, Thomas,' I stammer. I don't usually stammer, so that will give you some idea of my new emotional state. 'After Thomas à Becket.'

She ignores the sniggers coming from my classmates, which, of course, is her way of binding us closer together. 'Thank you, Thomas,' she says.

'How ya goin', *Thomas*?' I hear in stage whispers all around me.

But I don't care because I've discovered something. I've discovered that it's true. Those love stories on the telly that you hear about are true. They're not nauseating rubbish after all. They're real.

I think of my father and the Blonde One in the cafe and, just for a moment, I understand. Of course, what Dad is doing is really off. He's already got someone to take out for coffee and cake and to hold hands with. He's got his wife. My mum. But at some place, at some moment, he too looked up and saw ... saw one who was blonde, blue-eyed and a smasher.

For the first time since the two of us walked out in the middle of *The Gumnut Fairies* when I was three, my dad and I have something in common.

Except that I'm not cheating on anyone. And there lies the difference.

But now I will stand straight. I will project my voice. I will be heard at the back of the hall, in the next street. Why am I not the good knight or even the bad knight, or a king or even a courtier? Why am I not someone with more lines to say? However, I do have *one* line, and that means it will be necessary to attend every single rehearsal from now on.

I think of Zood with love.

At last the rehearsal begins. We're running late because there's been a lot of appreciating of Miss J Effington-Smythe by a lot of people. The Brain has been quoting Shakespeare and breathing from the diaphragm. Nigel is describing how he has designed not one spy screen, but two. And Mad-Dog is explaining the art of lowering a drawbridge.

Miss Effington-Smythe is smiling and dimpling and everyone is smiling and dimpling back, including all the girls. Except for Jemima, who is not smiling and dimpling because suddenly here is someone who is as pretty as she.

The rehearsal is underway. And it is professional from the first breath. We stand straight, we project, we wave our arms around, we sparkle with our eyes, with our bodies. With everything. And Miss J Effington-Smythe sparkles back. This is high professionalism. Sir has gone ape with happiness. Nobody remarks that we are overtime, nobody complains when Sir suggests we rehearse next weekend. In fact, we wonder if one weekend rehearsal is enough.

The rehearsal is over and Sir is calling everyone closer to hear some final words from the ruby rosebud lips of Miss J Effington-Smythe. There is so much cooperation that a couple of knights are sent flying off the stage. But they stagger up smiling, as they have landed next to the black-stockinged legs of Miss J Effington-Smythe.

There is silence while we watch her blue eyes glance

at her notes and then look up at us. We are told how excellent we are and how well we are projecting to the back of the hall. Though, she says, it's also nice to project to the person you're talking to on stage, as well. And then she gives a few excellent suggestions, such as how the prince and the Lady Imogen could perhaps wait until they're united in their rightful realm before they show everyone how very fond of each other they are. And such as, although the bad king is a very good bad king, it would be wise if he actually stuck to the script. For if you keep adding words of your own, she says, it can be very confusing for the others on the stage.

And then suddenly she's gone.

We pile out of the hall in the direction of the car park, where she is headed. Then we stop. Because she, too, has stopped—beside a little red Mazda. With golden curls dancing, she unlocks the door and proceeds to place a delicate, black-stockinged leg inside. Now, it surprises me to discover that I'm suddenly very interested in cars. Particularly in Mazdas. In fact, I see myself being quite an authority. So it seems appropriate that I should check out her car a bit. Make sure the wheels aren't falling off. That the bumper bar's screwed on, that sort of thing. The whole tribe trails along after me.

Miss J Effington-Smythe, oh Miss J Effington-Smythe ...

I give a little skip.

I notice, with annoyance, that several of the others are giving a little skip too.

Even Sir is heard whistling across the quadrangle.

Who would have believed it?

Who would have believed that I am now counting down the days, the hours, the minutes, to the next rehearsal?

But I am.

Full Rehearsal

Reveal, reveal, reveal . . .

Everywhere I go—under the shower, at the table, on my bike, in class, in bed, inside, outside—I whisper, mutter, speak, scream the *Word*. The nightmare is far from over. It has instead risen to mammoth proportions.

Snap! *Reveal.* Snap! *Relieve.* Snap! *Reveal.* Snap! *Relieve.*

And now, not only must I say the right word, but it must ignite the stage with fire and passion. *She* must see *me*, and me alone.

It's first thing in the morning. It's a full rehearsal, and this means we will be rehearsing on the set, which is finally ready. And *she* will be here.

The past three weeks of rehearsals have resulted in a very happy director and a very happy cast. It's now also a look-alike cast. That is, if you're a girl. The girls (except for Jemima) have gone curly. Even Angie, whose hair usually hangs straight as a curtain. They've also turned blonde. According to Angie, who is already blonde, the other girls have used cheap peroxide in their efforts to be the same as Miss Effington-Smythe.

It's amazing. It's Saturday morning, it's not even nine o'clock and I'm not even the first one here.

In the hall there's already a very cooperative scene. People are flexing their sword arms, making lunging movements, projecting their lines (*reveal, reveal, reveal*), and breathing from the diaphragm. Others are producing serious *clip-clop* sound effects with coconut shells. Everyone is directing their cooperative effort towards the centre back of the hall where Miss J Effington-Smythe is standing.

How to speak to her? How to get a minute alone with her?

(*Reveal, reveal, reveal.*)

Sir is clapping his hands, which means we are about to begin. He only has to do this once, because we are being so cooperative. But before we start, we are going to be instructed by Miss Effington-Smythe in the art of walking, sitting and bending down. The way these things are performed on stage, that is.

We spread out at the back of the hall and watch the demonstration. Sir's eyes gleam. Rarely has he witnessed such concentration. We watch her walk. Then we walk, holding our heads high (we have to, as there is a book balancing on each of our scones). We watch her sit. Then we lower ourselves into chairs, clamp our legs together, backs ramrod straight. She claps delicate little hands. She tells us that we are going to learn how to pick something up from the floor. Heads nod seriously. We rush about, looking for items to practise with. I spy a few half-dead flowers in a vase behind the curtain. One of them is still vaguely alive. A rose.

We bend with our knees, pluck things from the floor. Again and again. We could bend and pluck and sit and walk all day. But now she looks at her watch, tells us how brilliant we are and also that later she'll be coaching the knights in sword play.

Why aren't I a knight? I want to be a knight.

I do have a rose, though, in my hand.

A rose that is now in her hand.

'Thank you, Thomas.' She smiles.

Amid murmurs of 'Total dag', I join the others moving toward the stage.

Once again Sir claps his hands. We all take our places without a peep. I go to my spot which is stage right (which, if you're standing in the hall and facing the stage, means the left). I position myself behind the curtain. (*Reveal, reveal, reveal.*) I can see Miss Effington-Smythe at the centre back of the hall, pencil poised, through a chink in the curtain.

'From the top!' announces Sir, and he proceeds to stick his glasses on the end of his nose and pace up and down in the middle of the hall. And I'm betting this is so that a certain someone can watch him. And who can blame him? It is some audience. Even if it is only an audience of one.

Weasel, as the bad knight, strides onto the stage, heaves up his diaphragm, fixes his eye at the centre back and bellows, '"My mood is sombre, quiet and reflective ..."'

And we're away. By the time the bad king, who is really Mario, has projected his intention to banish the Lady Imogen (which is accompanied by *ahhhhhs* and *awwwwws* from the sound effects team), we think that perhaps Sir is right and that we are indeed big-time professionals.

'*Ahhh, awww, ooooh!*'

Each time the Lady Imogen puts her hand to her brow to indicate quiet despair (which she does for most of the play), the chorus swells.

'Not so loud!' screams Sir. But Lady Imogen's hand is at her brow again.

'*Ahhh, awwww, ooooh!*'

'"Lower the drawbridge!"' projects Mario-the-bad-king to the centre back of the hall.

Sir's face is getting redder. 'Turn around and face the thing!' he barks.

Mario twists around. '"Lower the drawbridge!"' he yells with his head turned hard enough left to still project to the centre back of the hall.

'Don't,' hisses Weasel.

'Don't what?' asks Mario.

'Don't lower the drawbridge.'

'It's alright, Sir,' Mad-Dog's head pops out from behind the curtain. 'I got a new chain.'

'"Lower the drawbridge,"' projects Mario again, and then adds in a stage whisper, 'How does the moron think we're gonna get in? Crawl up the walls? "Lower the drawbridge!"'

The drawbridge comes down. Very quickly. So quickly that it snaps clean off, knocking a couple of courtiers into the moat and clattering across the stage to the edge where it balances precariously for a second or two. Then falls off.

'Oh bum!'

'Angelica, good queens don't say bum.'

'Good queens don't have their legs sliced by flying draw-bridges.'

'Stage manager, remove the drawbridge,' bellows Sir, who is now sitting in his director's chair. He turns to the back of the hall. 'Little problem, ha, ha, ha.'

Reveal, reveal, reveal.

'Reveal what?' Foxy whispers at me from behind the curtain.

'I'm learning my lines.'

The Brain, as the good knight (who is the prince is disguise) comes on. '"Never fear, my dearest, I will not rest until—"'

'Hey, Sir!'

'Shut up, you!' bawls the good knight.

'Who spoke? Who's interrupting—'

'Us, Sir. We're in the moat.'

'Well, I can't help that. I didn't put you there.'

'The drawbridge did. We've been down here for ages.'

The Brain stalks across the stage, peers into the makeshift space below the drawbridge, roars 'Shut up!' and stalks back. '"Never fear, my dearest—"'

'Hey, Sir, can't we be saved, Sir? It'd be cool to be saved.'

Chook's head appears from behind the curtain. 'We can make good saving noises, Sir.'

'No, do you hear me? *No, no, no!*' Sir sends a limp smile to the centre back, where Miss J Effington-Smythe is taking notes. 'Continue!'

'"Never fear, my dearest, I will not rest until we are united forever in our rightful realm. This royal throne of kings . . ."'

The Brain is looking virtuous and very princely as he strides towards the gold-painted, jewel-encrusted throne. And as he sits he's supposed to say that one day the throne will be his. He sits with a princely flourish. There's the sound of ripping and tearing and very loud swearing as the throne splits in two and the prince sits on the floor with his feet up in the air. Which is hardly a pose that would appeal to Lady Imogen.

'There's no flipping chair!' yowls the virtuous prince.

'Where's the chair?' roars Sir. 'Stage manager, where's the chair?'

'What chair, Sir?'

'The canvas chair that goes under the cardboard, you—'

'It was there, Sir. I put it there.'

Then suddenly here it comes, sliding slap-bang into the middle of the stage. And at the same time there is a sudden movement of curtain and the face of Foxy appears around the edge of it.

'Sorry, Sir,' he says. 'There was a knot at the top. I had to get on a chair to untangle it and that was the only chair I could find. It came out quite nicely from under the cardboard. And because you're standing for a long time when you're a curtain puller I sat on it and forgot to put it back.'

I turn from watching this explanation to peep towards the back of the hall. Miss J Effington-Smythe has got a hanky up to her face. It seems she has a cold. This is not good. I stare harder. Then I see she's making the sort of body movements you make when you giggle. Her shoulders are shaking, her head is shaking. Her legs are wiggling.

'Continue,' says Sir, with a sigh.

The bad knights storm the castle, dispatching the sentries as they rush towards the portcullis across the drawbridge, which isn't there because it's still on the hall floor. Behind the curtain, Chook and his sound-effects team are making storming and dispatching and rushing noises. And the bad knights, led by Weasel, are approaching the portcullis with their bodies leaning to the right, because the portcullis bars have been nailed on at a slant.

'"The One whom you seek is amongst us."'

That is the cue for the portcullis to go up. But it doesn't. The knights stop. It's completely silent except for Chook going *clip-clop* with his coconut shells. The knights wait for something to happen.

'Give it a shove, ya nerd,' the stage manager says in a loud whisper.

Weasel reaches out and pushes, and in doing so gets his hand stuck between the nicely painted iron bars. Which are actually wood.

'He's got his hand stuck, Sir.'

'Then get it unstuck!'

'Ow!' yells Weasel.

'It won't unstick, Sir.'

'Hey, Sir!' Foxy's face pops out from behind the curtain. 'He could be a statue. We could have one on the other side too. Statues guarding the portcullis with their hands through the bars would look rather nice.'

'I'll be a statue with its hands through the bars,' says a voice from the moat.

'Stage manager, get his hand out of that thing!'

'Hey, Sir, my mother got a ring off her hand once with soap,' pipes up Matthew Wigg, the ever-helpful good king.

'Get soap. Get saws. Get anything . . .'

'Ow!' howls Weasel.

The backstage crew gets busy, and by the time they have finished there is very little left of the portcullis, which perhaps is not such a bad thing. Without it the knights have a much easier job of storming the castle and Weasel has his hand back, though a bit of his finger is missing.

While all this is happening, we don't hear anything from Sir. And I notice that Miss Effington-Smythe has her hanky up to her mouth again.

We're getting near the end of the play and the moment when I say my line (*reveal, reveal, reveal*). Which is after a sword fight that I won't describe, except to say The Brain's sword has just snapped.

'How can I play a hero with a sword that snaps like a matchstick every time I try to use it! Weasel's got the best sword, but *I'm* supposed to win the fight. So I should have the best sword. Hand it over.'

'But, Sir—' projects Weasel.

'Are you going to hand it over or not?'

'I like my sword.'

'I'll count to three,' snarls The Brain. 'One two . . .'

And when Weasel still doesn't move, The Brain does. They wrestle. This wrestling is accompanied by loud squeaks of pain from Weasel because of his sore hand.

'Here you are, ya wimp,' groans Weasel, tossing the sword at The Brain.

'Can we continue?' It's Sir's voice. He's still conscious.

Reveal, reveal, reveal.

It is here. My cue. Which is—

"The moment, at last, is come."

I step onto the stage.

'"Reveal yourself and flee,"' I bellow to the back of the hall.

I've done it! I've done it!

'Again, with more oomph,' calls Sir.

Oh no, please not again.

'"Reveal, reveal, reveal yourself and fleeee."'

'No, you only say reveal once.'

'"Reveal yourself and fleeee."'

I stride off stage.

And I want to say it again. I want to breathe with my diaphragm like no one has ever breathed before. I want to project to the far wall. To the oceans and the rivers. To the tops of the trees. To the mountain peaks. To her.

I peek through the chink in the curtain. Miss Effington-Smythe is smiling. Oh, to speak to her alone! I can feel vibrations coursing towards me from the centre back. She has responded to my fire and passion. She has . . .

She is going. The rehearsal is over.

I slink into the hall, search for her over the milling sea of heads and spot her making for the door.

Suddenly there's a scream.

'What?' Sir wheels in horror and charges in the direction of the scream.

We all follow, and arrive at the back of the hall in time to see Bugs yanking something from a delicate black stocking. He holds up his second-best centipede, Ron, which has been making its way up Miss Effington-Smythe's left leg. And Miss Effington-Smythe is shaking herself and jumping up and down and peering up sleeves and collars and skirt in case one of Ron's friends is around.

Still quivering, Miss Effington-Smythe looks for her scattered notes which are now being scooped up by a couple of fleet-footed nerds. And then she heads for the door.

Sir pushes through the crowd.

We watch as he walks her to her car with his arm around her.

On faces everywhere I read exactly what I'm feeling.

Our eyes glint with venom.

J.E.S.

I'm not by nature very tidy. And there are those who claim that I'm not too clean either—such as my mum, who says I'm plain dirty. According to her, I suffer from aversions. Aversions to cleaning my nails, aversions to washing my hair, aversions to changing my socks, aversions to tidying my room. I used to have an aversion to cleaning my teeth, but the dentist cured me of that.

It's not that I object to cleanliness, I simply don't see the point of it. I mean, five minutes after you're squeaky clean you begin to get dirty again. The only way to remain pristine is to spend your life under the hose.

However, my nature has undergone a change. I am now a front runner in the Cleanliness and Tidiness Stakes. And I'll tell you the reason why. It's because of a certain person who wears a delicate little flower-like skirt and black stockings that the new me has been born. And being a new me has changed things. For a start, Mum has stopped mentioning her list of my aversions. I guess she's thinking that her nagging has at last paid off.

Anyway, what happened was that the moment I picked

up Miss Effington-Smythe's dropped script and eye-balled the state of my own fingernails, my thinking changed. On that day I knew my days of being a pig were over. I am changed. I wash. I scrub. I polish my boots. I change my socks, I shampoo my hair, leather shoes have replaced grey runners, the shirt's in the wash if there's the slightest speck, I floss my teeth, I carry a comb, I *use* a comb . . .

I am in love and because I am in love, I have changed. I am plucking rosebuds from people's rose gardens. I am perched on ladders watching sunsets. I am in harmony with birds and butterflies and the buzzing bees. I smile in the street at little old ladies and snotty-nosed kids. I am exercising. I am eating body-building vegetables as well as having nightmares (*reveal, reveal, reveal*) and going mad. And this last bit is my creative genius coming out, because every creative genius you've ever heard of is mad.

I am also writing the most excellent poetry.

Little snail upon a flower
Dreaming hour after hour

And I scrawl on everything from porcelain to plastic the initials JES: J Effington-Smythe. I carve these adored letters on tree trunks, gateposts, fences, fireplaces. I write them with the foam that froths from my regularly-taken bubble baths.

And I sing. Not in tune, but loudly.

There was a time when I would have spent the entire music lesson training centipedes under the desk. But now I sing.

'I'm singing, Sir.'

'I know. We all know. The whole school knows. The residents of the northern suburbs know.'

It's nice to give pleasure to people.

To add to this, I hate to admit it, I'm doing my homework. I even got an A.

Of course, what nobody knows is that I will do anything—slave at homework, perfect every task, polish every toenail, deposit every banana skin, get a good Term Three report—anything. Just to impress her. Just for one glimpse of the gorgeous dimpled smile of Miss J Effington-Smythe.

J ...? J ...? Jennifer? Jacqueline? Julia? Jill? Josephine? Jessica? Jane? Joanna? No.

Night after night, when I'm not asleep having nightmares, I lie awake and wonder what the J stands for. Until suddenly I know. Japonica, of course. It has to be. Sweet, delicate and softly perfumed like the flower ... Japonica Effington-Smythe, I love you.

Your eyes are blue
Hair golden hue
Your turned up nose
A budding rose
Your tiny dimple
Free of pimple
I love you
From you know who.

I am a literary giant.

We are now well into the fourth week of rehearsing. And, for the second time, Sir has called for a weekend rehearsal. Not a soul has squeaked a complaint.

Today I will speak to her. I must find a way. I consider letting down her tyres so that I can come to her rescue. Or hiding in the boot of her little red Mazda. Or staging a cramp-in-the-left-leg attack next to the front wheels.

But today she has arrived late and left early and though, as soon as we finish, I make a lightning dash for the car park, she and her little red Mazda have gone.

'Gone to training,' gasps Mario, who has come charging along behind.

'Who has?'

'She has.'

'Where?'

'Dunno. But Billy Opman's playing.'

'Billy Opman?'

'That's what she told Sir. Weasel heard her.'

I charge off in search of Bugs. Bugs is into football big-time. His room's smothered in posters of football stars shooting goals, saving goals, slide tackling ... And when he's not at school you're bound to find him dressed up in blue and white. Sometimes he even wears a blue and white T-shirt under his school shirt.

It's afternoon recess. Bugs is under the magnolia in the quad, with a couple of others, chomping chips.

'Bill Opman's training today,' I say.

'So?'

'You going?'

'Training's not open to the public,' he retorts, as though I should know.

'Where do they train?'

'Where does who train?'

'Whoever Billy Opman trains with.'

'At the stadium, of course. What do *you* want to know for?'

'What's Billy Opman doing training with the local team?' asks Foxy, who's just fronted up.

'Just 'cos he's a World Cup player doesn't mean he doesn't play with his local team,' says Bugs with a touch of the know-all.

'And what time do they start?'

'Early,' says Bugs, then pauses and shoots me a look. 'What are you up to, anyway?' he asks.

On the Trail

If Bugs is right and training sessions aren't open to the public, then why is *she* going?

I don't understand it.

I still haven't found a way to talk to her alone. She wants me to, I know. I can feel it. But I need a proper excuse. Then suddenly I have an idea.

The bell's gone for the end of school and we're clambering down the stairs from the classroom. Sir is staggering behind. He doesn't look as sprightly these days. Also he's starting to go bald.

I flatten myself against the wall and wait for him to catch up. We descend together.

'The play's going well, Sir,' I say.

'You think so, Tom?'

'Yeah, except—'

'Except what?'

'I'm a bit worried about my line.'

'You're doing fine.'

'I made that mistake the other day. And it worried you, I could tell.'

'Tom, it's nice to know that you're conscientious,' he says. 'But I'm not worried, so you shouldn't be.'

'Problem is, Sir, I *am* worried. And I'm thinking some private tuition might stop me worrying. After all, there's only two and a bit weeks to go.'

'Don't remind me.'

'I know you're busy so I wondered if that lady . . . what's-her-name . . . might be able to—'

We've reached the ground floor. Sir stops and looks at me strangely. 'You're the fifth person today who's made the same request. Your friend Foxy insists he needs advice on pulling the curtains.'

I leave Sir staggering off, then look for Weed and give him a yell. We heave up our bikes and take off, yakking, as always, as we go.

Weed peels off at his house and I ride on towards my house. Though today I make a small detour past the stadium. And as I arrive there I'm wondering, what did Bugs mean by 'early'? *Right now* is early, but there's no sign of cars outside or anyone hanging around. Perhaps 'early' means earlier than when the match usually starts. But what time does the match start?

If it was cricket I'd know the answers to all of this . . .

I go home.

'We're having an early dinner,' warbles my mother. 'Your father's got a meeting.'

I reckon Dad's overdoing the 'meeting' thing. He'll have to come up with something more imaginative if he's going to keep sneaking off for coffee and cake. My mother is not stupid.

An early dinner, however, will suit me, because I'm going back to the stadium. Not to hang around outside on my own, of course, as that would look pretty stupid. But if I'm hanging around with a dog . . .

I lean against the kitchen bench, watch Mum slice potatoes.

'We had this vet at school today,' I say, making it up as I go. 'He was going on about dogs. About exercise being good for their hearts and their muscles and—'

'I've been telling you that for ages.' Mum eyeballs Gloop. 'Look at him, lazy and overweight.'

Gloop wags his tail. Looks sad.

Over dinner my mother goes on and on about my climb up the academic ladder—due mainly to getting that A for homework. My father nods his head and continues to eat. He's obviously got his mind on other things. But I'm not going to think about *other things*. Not today. Not now.

'Walkies, Gloop?'

Gloop slinks under the table.

'He's forgotten what the word means,' my father remarks.

I grab the lead and we take off.

Bugs is right. Training isn't open to the public. But it now must be 'early', because training is definitely on. At least, something is on. A few cars are parked around. A couple of people are hanging around too, probably hoping to get a glimpse of the World Cup player. One of them is wearing blue and white.

I yank Gloop along the sweep of lawn that circles the stadium. I pull him away from a nice-smelling tree to turn the corner and . . . there it is. Her car. I know the number plate *off by heart*.

My legs go funny, my hands wobble. Here is her car, and this means that she is here too.

Today is Wednesday. Wednesday is training day. It is a day I will remember.

I drag Gloop back to the entrance. I sit on the grass. Gloop sits on the grass. How long do these training sessions last?

After waiting for what seems like forever, there's movement. Two men come out, followed by two more.

I leap up. Heave Gloop up.

And there she is. She's talking to a man and a woman by the entrance.

Now the three of them are heading around the stadium to where her car's parked.

I move too. I walk at an angle so that I'll cross their path.

'Thomas!' She smiles. She looks at Gloop. 'And who are you?'

Who is he? I can't remember. 'A dog,' I stammer.

She bends down, ruffles shaggy ears. 'You're a lovely fellow,' she says.

Gloop sits, lifts up his paw. It's his party trick.

She laughs, walks on.

'Bye, Thomas,' she calls. 'See you on Saturday.'

I can't answer. My heart is beating so hard it's bashing my ears.

The Publicity Campaign

It hurts me to have to admit it, but my father is right. You *do* learn from books and, if you're serious about it, you can learn big-time. Like I have. Now I must know as much about football as Bugs does. Could he tell me, for example, the name of the new defender they've brought out from Brazil? Well ... he probably could, but you get what I mean.

For the past two days at recess time, lunchtime and after school, I have buried myself in the library. It's terrible to think that I've been wasting my energies on cricket all these years, when here before me is the game that's played in *every country of the world*.

Oh, Japonica Effington-Smythe, you are so right to love football!

Also, I look rather elegant in blue and white.

And now it is Saturday and rehearsal is over.

We are gathered around Miss J (for Japonica) Effington-Smythe and she is telling us about our publicity campaign. Everybody is muscling in, because everybody wants praise from Miss Effington-Smythe ... including me. But I am far from pleased to observe that I am not the only one looking clean. Everyone is trying to outdo everyone else. Bugs is in his best blue and white shirt, even though it prickles his skin. The Brain is colour-coordinated in green and gold. Even Mad-Dog is looking beautiful in red leather. Which, not so long ago, he said made him look like a gangster and he would not be seen dead in it. And Weed is eyeing me strangely, as he has never before seen me looking so elegant.

Silence descends as Japonica—that is, Miss Effington-Smythe—starts to speak.

Who, she wants to know, is imaginative and energetic enough to mount a successful publicity campaign?

There is much waving of hands, and voices yelling *me, me, me!*

Sir is almost jumping with joy at this level of cooperation.

I shove to the front. 'My mum's a university lecturer,' I bellow.

Miss Effington-Smythe looks at me, one eyebrow raised as if to say, what has that got to do with anything.

'In advertising,' I add inventively.

So, over the top of a very ugly chorus of 'pig's ear' and other rude expressions, she asks me to pick a hard-working and enthusiastic team. Now, as you know, Mad-Dog is the printer of posters (as well as the puller-up of drawbridges), and Bugs is the assistant to the printer of posters and Weed is the putter up of posters. In fact, while I was reading up on football in the library, they've spent their lunchtimes in the art room with paper and marker pens drawing up very excellent posters, and then photocopying them in the office. So, of course, they are the obvious choice to help me advertise the school play. Also, it just so happens that they are my friends.

We are all very enthusiastic about mounting a successful publicity campaign, so after rehearsal we gather at Weed's place to plot and plan. Fortunately Weed has remembered everything that Miss Effington-Smythe told us this morning. And now he is in considering mode and thinking laterally.

Weed: You've gotta have TV. And radio. And the papers.

Mad-Dog: And we have to put our posters up.

Weed: And we need jelly beans.

Me: Whatcha mean, 'jelly beans'?

Weed: Guessing how many. If people guess right, they get two tickets.

Bugs: What for?

Weed: The play, you moron. Twenty cents a guess.

Bugs: Where do we get the jelly beans?

Weed: From Miss Peabody, ya dummy. She'll go ape when we give her a ticket. I'll bet not too many people invite her out to a big-time theatrical experience.

We immediately push off in the direction of Miss Peabody's shop.

Weed is right, in one respect. In fact, Miss Peabody is quite enthusiastic about giving us jelly beans because she has quite a few packets of them that are past their use-by date. She also has a jar full of black jelly beans which she had ordered and that nobody wants, and she's happy to offload them onto us. However, she suddenly remembers that she has to be out on the night of the play and she is very, very sorry that she won't be able to make it.

Monday morning, armed with a jar of stale and mostly black jelly beans, we get to school and count them. By the time they are transferred to a bigger jar they are not only stale but sticky and finger marked as well.

At lunchtime we make for the primary school across the road. The infants' teacher is expecting us. Sir has rung her to ask if we could come over and, while doing so, has also mentioned the brilliance of his play. And because Sir has offered to give her a free ticket, she has said yes, we can do the guessing game with her pupils. And she has worded up the little kids, who are now racing towards us with their twenty-cent pieces.

Before you know it, we're weighed down with quite a few bucks.

For little kids, they make some pretty good guesses. The problem is that none of them want a ticket to the play. Not even the winner. He just wants the jelly beans. We point out that the beans are stale, but he still wants them. We tell him they might make him sick but he says he doesn't care. We decide it's time to start the heavy-arm tactics but now he's looking as though he's going to scream. So we let him go and hope that he will vomit nonstop for a week.

At afternoon recess we gather together again.

Even though I'm the main publicity person, I ask Weed what we should do next. Weed says putting up the posters is next, and I say, 'where?' And he says on posts and Mad-Dog adds that we should also put them on stations. Bugs wants to know what sort of stations and Weed considers this and says railway stations, bus stations, ambulance stations, fire stations and any other kind of stations you can think of.

We decide to put up posters in the afternoon after rehearsal.

At rehearsal, we talk about costumes. The kings and queens and Lady Imogen look-alikes have already been working on their costumes for ages, but now it's the turn of the guards and knights. Because I'm a guard I have to wear chain mail. All guards and knights do, though the knights will have geranium leaves on theirs. Apparently that's how they went about in the twelfth century. Sir has looked into this in a big way. The knights and guards are handed rolls of grey canvas and black curtain rings and patterns, and told to take them home and bring them back as tunics of chain mail. As you know, chain mail is nothing but a tunic with iron rings all over it, though our rings will be plastic. As a guard, I also have to wear a helmet and stockings ... but that's too painful to talk about.

After school I roll up my bundle of canvas and curtain rings and head for Weed's place. We gather up our poster-pasting gear, and head out.

We walk for ages. You'd think finding a blank wall would be easy. It isn't. But at last, as we go past the back of a building, Weed yells, 'Here's one.'

It's a lovely wall with nice red bricks. Clean, too. The posters look excellent when they're up, even though they're a bit crooked and there's glue oozing down the brickwork.

It's when we're packing up our glue and brushes that Bugs, who's been doing a bit of investigating, points out that our posters are stuck to the back of the police station. He also mentions that policemen are walking our way.

Well, it turns out that these two policemen are deadheads. They're not coming to the play. Though they *do* come to the conclusion that unless every scrap of poster—and that includes the rivers of glue—is removed from the wall, we're in for a talking to. And they go on to say how very lucky we are that the police feel so loving towards young people, or it could have been a lot worse.

So now, under cover of darkness, armed with a bucket of glue and a roll of posters, we make for the train station instead. It's not a manned station and there's no one on the platform. We decide we've found the perfect spot and get to work. Which is a mistake, because soon the graffiti painters arrive and they are not happy to see us. They carry spray cans. They survey the five posters that we've pasted on each of the signs bearing the name of the station. Then they stroll slowly and nastily towards us.

1st graffiti painter: What's that garbage?

Mad-Dog: (with shaking voice) Our school play. We ... um ...

2nd graffiti painter: (ripping poster from sign) Garbage.

Weed: Hey—

1st graffiti painter: (taking a step closer) You say somethin'?

Weed: Nup. Nup.

Me: He didn't say a word.

And he certainly won't say a word for a while, either,

because the third graffiti painter, who has been ripping down the posters, has slapped a strip of torn poster over Weed's mouth. It covers his mouth, his nose and his chin. If we stay around any longer it's likely that we'll all end up covered in bits of poster, which now lie shredded on the ground, so we make a quick exit. By this time so much glue has sloshed from the bucket there is only just enough left for us to put up a poster on Miss Peabody's shop window.

Then Mad-Dog sneezes and trips over with the bucket. So now there's no glue left for Miss Peabody's window. Bugs steps in the spilt glue and he's walking like he's on the moon. In the end, the only things that have posters stuck to them is us. And that's only poster parts.

And now I heave myself and my chain-mail kit home to my mother. She hums and haws at great length over the canvas and curtain rings. I suspect she is making these noises because she thinks my one line should be delivered by someone whose chain mail is a bit classier than everyone else's. It turns out I'm right.

But I won't know for sure till the following afternoon.

It's the next morning, we're on our way to school and Weed is ranting on about how the media sucks. The print media in particular, because the local paper isn't interested in our play.

'We've got a hundred school plays on this month,' they told him. 'If you can come up with an angle we'll think about it.'

'You'd expect more from a newspaper editor, wouldn't

you?' argues Weed. 'I thought they were supposed to encourage community spirit.'

At morning recess, while we are unsuccessfully looking for an angle, we consider how to crack the big ones.

Weed: We gotta crack the big ones.

Mad-Dog: What big ones?

Weed: TV.

Bugs: And radio.

Mad-Dog: How we gonna crack them?

It's lunchtime and we're at Weed's place, because we've got permission to leave school on account of the importance of the publicity campaign. That's when we get our idea. It's given to us by Weed's mum. It's Weed's mum's day off and she's making poppyseed bread and supervising us. The radio is tuned to a local station. The topic is Neo-Nazism.

'Hear that?' says Weed's mum. 'It's right on our doorstep. Yesterday those people broke up a local branch meeting in Greenvale. Just around the corner. This is hot stuff.'

I'm about to point out that Greenvale is not just around the corner, unless she means the corner of the next state, when Weed gets an idea.

Weed: We could say there's a Neo-Nazi meeting at the school.

Bugs: When's the next rehearsal?

Me: Tonight. Seven o'clock.

Weed: Okay, so radio reporters'll come charging in thinking they're going to expose a Neo-Nazi meeting, and there we'll be with our swords and coconut shells. And the journos'll decide that, because they're already there, they'd better do some reporting so they'll at least look like they're doing their job properly.'

We're very proud of Weed for thinking laterally, and the thought of having the play advertised on radio is very pleasant indeed. Though, with all this publicity we're bound to get, it's likely that the play will have to run nonstop for six months, rather than for just one night.

Weed looks up the number for the radio station. 'Who's going to call them?' he asks.

Bugs says, 'It was your idea.'

'I sound like a kid,' replies Weed.

This is true. Because that's what he is. It's what we all are.

Weed is looking at me like he's running out of lateral thinking. 'You,' he says.

I go to the phone. I ring the number he's given me. I explain about the meeting that will be held this evening. The man at the radio station is impressed. He thanks me for being cooperative. Then he asks some very unnecessary and personal questions. I have to hang up quickly.

Now all we have to do is charge back to school. And wait.

It is home-time. And by now we have remembered that there is no rehearsal this evening because something else will be on in the hall. I try calling the radio station again to tell them the Neo-Nazi meeting is off, but I don't know the name of the man I spoke to. The man I am speaking to now thinks what I'm telling him is a joke (which it is) and hangs up in my ear.

So we hotfoot it home and hope for the best.

Which is wasted energy, because my mother has arrived

home with gold curtain rings and purple-coloured canvas.

'I'm not going to wear that!' I squeak. 'No one wears purple and gold! Not even Lady Imogen.'

But my mother is already whirring away on her sewing machine and singing loudly. There's no use trying to argue with my mother when she sings.

The next morning we hear that things did not go well the night before. We hear that reporters from the radio station, as well as journalists and a photographer from the local paper, turn up at the school and find a Parents Club Fundraising Meeting being chaired by the deputy principal. With the result that he and the school committee end up at the police station (the reporters having tipped off the police), with everyone looking very confused and doing a lot of lateral thinking.

But from this comes success. The school is headline material and there's a mention of the play. In small print at the bottom. But that's something.

Crash Landing

Because of all the publicity trauma, I haven't given my father a thought. And this I must do. So after school I ring Gran, whose help I want in the 'get father' department, and who's been off on a bus trip somewhere with her cronies.

'Hi, Gran.'

'Hello, Pet.'

'How was your trip?'

'I had a lovely time. The first day we ... blah blah blah ...'

I let her go on for a bit, then I tell her I want to see her.

Fortunately, Gran would love to see me, too. And she would love to see Weed as well. She suggests Friday after school.

'Does Reed like sausage rolls?' she asks before hanging up.

In the meantime it's only Wednesday and Wednesday means football training. I have made up my mind that tonight I will say to Miss Effington-Smythe: 'I must talk to you ... Japonica.'

But what would I need to talk to her about? Perhaps I can say that I have an idea to make the play more ... more *something*. This *something* is something I'll have to work on.

Dinner comes, and so does my father with a nonstop story demonstrating the idiocy of the human race. It's a case he's working on. Where two people are battling over who will be getting the squillions after their divorce, the wife or the husband. And each has promised to kill the other if they're the one who doesn't end up with the dough.

'And then,' my father says, 'in the middle of it all *she* gets some disease and suddenly all *he* wants to do is hold her hand and bring her back to health. She gets better. He gets golf clubs. And the squillions are given to the poor.'

Do they have kids, I want to know.

'Aren't you taking the dog for a walk?' is the reply.

How does Dad know this? Does Mum tell Dad what I tell her?

I saddle up Gloop and off we go.

We get to the stadium.

I'm right. Training is on. There are even a couple more cars in the car park this week. As well as the little red Mazda.

I plonk down on the grass to wait, and rehearse what I'm going to say. I look at Gloop. 'His name is Gloop,' I repeat for the fifteenth time.

My watch ticks on. And on.

Finally I scramble to my feet. I yank up Gloop. People have appeared at the entrance and are moving off towards their cars.

I start to walk, to drag Gloop this way and that, to look casual and accidentally passing by.

I pass two men chatting by the gate. One is in the team colours of blue and white. He's tall and bronzed. His hair is blonde. He looks like a hero out of my myths and legends book.

'See you, Bill,' says his companion.

Bill? *Billy Opman*!

Now *she's* there. And ... she's talking to him! And they're walking off together!

They're coming towards me. I don't move. I can't. She's not looking at me. She only sees Billy Opman, who is holding her hand. She is goggling at him so much that she nearly walks straight into me. 'Oh, hello, Thomas ...'

I won't refer to her dimples at the moment if you don't mind.

She goggles at the hero again. 'Darling,' she says, 'this is Thomas, who's in the play I was telling you about. Look, Thomas, you can be the first to know.'

She takes her hand out of her jacket pocket and thrusts a great ugly diamond in front of my nose.

The bronze-and-blonde hero gives me a nod, then turns back to her. 'Come on, Joan, we'll be late,' he says.

What? Who?

Joan!

It's really terrible to see a grown boy cry.

Her name will not be mentioned again. From now on, she has ceased to exist. In any case, apart from anything else, who could be the soul mate of anyone called *Joan*?

I'm not going to say any more. I'm not going to tell you how I feel. Except that I'm probably going to die of a broken heart. Quite soon.

As I drag myself and Gloop home I know that this will be the case.

Except that it's not. For within moments I'm going through the second stage of heartbrokenness, which is anger. Something on a padded hanger smacks me in the face as I walk in the door. It is a coat of chain mail. A purple one. With gold rings glittering all over it.

My mother is smiling. 'You'll be the star of the show in that.'

I let out an almighty howl. I lunge at the thing. I yank it from its padded frame. I rip and tear and shred until the curtain rings are bouncing around on the floor.

'Goodness.' My mother has sat down and is looking at me over her glasses. 'Goodness,' she repeats. She views her shredded handiwork. 'It must be the artistic temperament.'

She contemplates this for a moment, then suddenly she picks up something, hurls it, and starts ranting and raving. About the money she's spent, the time she's spent and how she is not, repeat *not*, going to make another.

Especially not another made of ugly grey and black.

I stagger upstairs, dragging my artistic temperament and second-stage heartbreak with me.

Before I repeat that a Certain Person will never be referred to again, I must report that there is bound to be a most welcome side-benefit to heartbrokenness. You'll be pleased to know that everything will soon be right back to normal. My room'll be a mess. My socks'll stink. I'll get C– for my homework. And any word with more than two syllables will be struck from my vocabulary.

Oh, and football sucks.

Further Doings on the Home Front

There is a third stage to heartbreak, and this stage is nastiness. And since this is the stage I am now experiencing, my thoughts again focus on my father. Why should I suffer alone?

It is Thursday. Dad will remember this Thursday as the day of his unmasking.

However, in considering how to unmask him, my thoughts turn to the Blonde One. And to the story my father told last night at dinner. I'm thinking of that story and I'm wondering whether the reason that the husband and wife in Dad's story wanted to kill each other might have been due not to the squillions, but to the existence of a Blonde One.

And suddenly an idea is born.

It is *she* I must tackle, not my father. I must make her see what could result from what she is doing. I must make her feel guilty. So guilty that she won't even consider holding a certain hand again for a long time. Like forever.

After some lateral thinking, I decide I will tell the Blonde One that my mother is sick. And that if my mother doesn't have a certain loving hand to hold onto, she will die. I will add that if this happens, it will be the *Blonde One's* fault. And that she will most likely be punished, just like bad people are punished in my myths and legends book.

This I will tell her.

However, I don't want *him* to catch me doing this. Dad will need to be somewhere other than where I and the Blonde One will be. He will have to be *not* in his office, because that's the only place where I know I'll be able to find *her*.

And what do you know! On this day my father will be interstate studying up on some big-time crook.

I get though the day, and in the afternoon after school I'm in William Street in the city. I'm looking at the Supreme Court on one side of the street and at my father's chambers on the other. In front of his building rises a sculpture that reads '461', and which is an address known to a great many criminals.

I go over my lines, just as great actors do before making their entrance. Then I go into the building and take the lift to the twelfth floor.

It's silent up here. Serious stuff is going on behind the heavy oak panelling. Barristers not only have an army of secretaries, but they have clerks as well, who, judging by the to-ing and fro-ing along the heavy pile carpet, do most of the work. Leaving barristers to go out for coffee and cake.

'Hello, Tom!'

It's Joyce, Dad's secretary, folders flapping like wings under each arm. 'How's school? Your dad's out of the office.'

Then off she trots.

I sit at a little table. On level twelve there are lots of little tables with newspapers for people to read, and over which they can observe the passing traffic. And it passes continually. And sometimes very young and very blonde passing traffic it is too.

I wait. But in a minute Joyce will reappear and wonder what I'm doing. So I get up, wander along corridors, around corners, along more corridors. Back into the lift and down to the clerks' office on the first floor.

'Hello, Tom. Dad's away,' says the first person I see.

This is not going well. It may be a complete waste of time. I had assumed the Blonde One would be working in Dad's chambers. Barristers don't have time to go around finding blondes and chatting them up in wine bars. They simply make do with the blondes that are already in their own offices.

I start towards the stairwell that leads to the ground floor.

I turn. A lift has hissed open. And the Blonde One steps out and walks towards me.

Panic!

She gets closer, she is passing me.

'I've seen you,' I blurt out.

She stops and turns. 'Are you talking to me?'

I nod.

'Who are you?'

Who am I? Who am I? 'Er ... Tom. Michael McCann's dad ... um ... er ... boy. Son.'

'Oh?' She smiles.

'I saw you.'

Her smile doesn't falter. She looks at me expectantly.

'With him.'

'Yes.' She stares me right in the eye. Doesn't even blush.

'I've got a message—'

'I don't think he's in today.'

I go on. 'It's my mum. She's been admitted again.' I'm shaking a bit. A lot, actually, but hopefully she will be thinking this is because of my high level of concern for my mum.

'Come here,' she says. She draws me over to a couch. I sink into cream leather. She is very close.

'I'm Kate.'

'You're with my dad?'

'I'm one of his colleagues.' So she's a barrister too! 'And your mum?'

'Er . . . in the Prince Albert.'

'Is it serious?'

'Yeah, oh yeah, they're real worried.'

'What is it?'

'Depression and . . . well . . .'

She's scrabbling for her phone. 'He must be told—'

He's given her his number!

'No!' I gasp.

'He must—'

I think quickly. 'If you tell him, that could make it worse. That's what they said.'

A pause. 'Oh dear, oh dear . . .'

In a minute she's going to ask why I'm there. But instead, she says, 'I've never met your mum . . .' (I'll bet!) 'Oh dear, poor Mike.' (Mike!)

She's going on. 'I think your dad's great.' (Gotcha!) 'He's one of the kindest people I know.' She pauses. 'You see, I've been there too ... it's terrible, depression is. My mum was killed in a car crash ...' And she's off and talking. She doesn't let me get a word in. 'I was sitting here, on this very seat, crying. Mike saw me and took me for coffee. He told me that this shouldn't stop us from getting married ...'

What!

I begin to shake. I think I'm going to throw up. I wish I am anywhere but here.

I leap to my feet. I bolt to the stairwell. I catch a glimpse of her startled expression as I go. I hurtle down the stairs and charge into the street. I stumble off the pavement and into the gutter. I manage to stagger onto a tram. I clutch the strap as it grinds up the hill.

I think of Mad-Dog and Mad-Dog's mum and how sad they are that his dad has heaved off with another lady to a thirty-sixth floor. And I think how angry and hurt they must have been at the beginning. And how they probably fronted up to whoever-she-was and tried to make her feel guilty for what she was doing. And I understand why they would have done that. Because that's what I've done ... and instead of feeling better, I feel worse.

A man opposite is staring at me. I want to punch him in the face. I want to punch the whole world in the face.

I want to cry.

I get home. I sit on my bed. I stare at the wall.

I hear Mum come in. She calls up to me. I hear her go to the kitchen.

I wish I was somewhere else. I wish I was someone else. I wish I was dead.

Life sucks.

I hear the phone ring.

Mum calls. 'It's Dad. For you.'

I lurch downstairs. Pick up the receiver. 'Hello.'

'I'm pleased you're home. Wanted a word . . .'

His voice sounds funny. I say, 'You sound funny.'

'I'm in a taxi coming from the airport . . . straight on, driver.' There's the sound of papers rustling. He's probably reading the newspaper at the same time as directing the taxi driver and talking to me.

'I've just heard the most extraordinary thing,' he says. 'Seems you made a visit to my chambers this afternoon.'

I realise that the Blonde One has rung him. She's described every word that was said.

'Tom, are you still there?'

Something's happened to my diaphragm. It's gone. I can't breathe.

'And it seems you made an extraordinary claim.' More rustling of paper. 'You must realise, Tom, that you've got to be very careful about what you say when barristers are around. And even what you say when they're *not* around, as the case may be. Barristers gather information, Tom. They study the information and then they draw conclusions.'

A squeak.

'And I'm currently drawing conclusions regarding the information I gathered today concerning your visit to my chambers. You follow me?'

Another squeak.

'Good. Left here, thank you driver ...'

I hang up. I sit on a chair. There was something strange about his voice, and it wasn't because he was in a taxi using a mobile phone. And so I am now drawing my own conclusions.

He's protecting *her*.

Dress Rehearsal

I chew on a single sliver of wheat bran, that being all the breakfast I can eat. Mum is worried. Should she ring the doctor? I think laterally and explain that for the last couple of days Mad-Dog has been splurging big at Miss Peabody's and sharing it with his mates. I list all the junk food I have eaten. Mum tut-tuts and sighs with relief.

The sliver of wheat bran swallowed, I take off for school.

Today is Dress Rehearsal. Dress Rehearsal is different from Full Rehearsal, and also from a Full Dress Rehearsal. Dress Rehearsal is where you try out your costumes to see if they fit.

And my costume doesn't fit. It doesn't even exist.

However, Chook's mum has made two costumes. A small one for a little guard and an enormous one for either a brontosaurus-size guard or for two middle-sized guards joined together. It was very cooperative of Chook's mum to do this because, as a sound-effects man, Chook doesn't have to get dressed up at all.

I am too big for the small one but the other does very nicely provided it is folded around me a couple of times.

And Mrs Throsby, who is helping out, has found some Velcro which she and Jenny, who is in charge of costumes, are attaching to my tunic. The problem is, the bits aren't long enough and pop open when I move, which means today I'll have to be tacked up. Jenny adds Velcro to her list of things to buy.

The result of the tacking up is that I look like a very strong and hefty guard. But since guards are supposed to be tough, this is probably not such a bad thing. And when I see myself in the mirror I must admit the chain mail looks excellent. Not only that, but I jingle as I walk along. As do all of those who are covered in bouncing black curtain rings. And it sounds very tuneful.

You'll notice that I appear to be acting quite cool. I am not, in fact, feeling cool. I'm feeling mega-stressed. I am also angry. And sad. And this means that if anyone says anything nice to me, I'll probably cry.

And I wonder if Mum's not right. That I am indeed a great actor. Because even though his heart might be breaking, an actor still has to tread the boards. Which is what I am somehow managing to do.

Weed has spent some time considering my situation, as I have told him of the disastrous journey to my father's chambers. It is Weed who has advised me to act cool. I tell him that I am. And I go on to remind him about seeing Grandma this afternoon and suggest we should get together to plan what we're going to say.

Weed agrees. And he points out that grandmas are not only wise, but have a lot of life experiences that they are pleased to share if you nag them enough.

I wonder about this, as it is my grandma who does most of the nagging.

'What if she can't think of a plan?' I ask.

'Then we take desperate measures,' says Weed.

'What desperate measures?'

But Weed is thinking.

So, as I said, I'm acting cool.

I will forget the man who would be my father. I will forget his Blonde One.

And I will forget the other one, She-Who-Will-Not-Be-Spoken-Of. I will forget delectable lips and flower-like skirts, and legs in black stockings that slip so delicately into little red Mazdas.

I will.

It is now ten o'clock.

Sir has walked onto the stage. He claps his hands. He reminds us that in seven more sleeps we will be treading the boards.

The rehearsal is about to start. She, who will not be spoken of, has arrived. All the props (short for properties, which is another word for swords and stuff) are in place. And there are jugs of water backstage because The Brain has watched Laurence Olivier, a very famous actor, on a DVD sipping litres of water before treading the boards. And since The Brain can't bear to be upstaged by anyone (including big-time Laurence Olivier), he is gulping down water by the bucketful.

'From the top!' bawls Sir, which means shut up and get on with it.

Weasel goes on, looking very dashing in his chain mail,

which tinkles musically, and starts projecting (though I'll refrain from mentioning in which direction). '"My mood is sombre, quiet and reflective . . ."'

He does it brilliantly and the moronic play is off to a very good start. I have to admit that although everybody knows how pathetic the play is, everybody is taking their parts seriously.

I take up my position behind the curtain and start to read a book. That's showing them how cool I am.

I eventually stop reading, for no one is admiring my coolness, and I start to concentrate on the play instead, which, to everyone's amazement, is going along quite nicely. Everything on the stage looks bright and beautiful, including Nigel's spy screen that the bad king is hiding behind, waiting patiently—through a lot of very well-projected speeches—to be knifed in the gut.

The Brain strides up to the screen in a very princely fashion and cries, '"Dead for a ducat, dead."'

No one is really sure what a ducat is except that they're always dead for one in plays by Shakespeare. The Brain begins thrusting his sword into the bad king very nicely and in time with Chook's choir's sound effects.

'*Haaa!*'

'*Errrrrrrrrrrrr!*'

'*Ha ha ha!*'

'*Errrrrrrrrrrrrrrrrrrrrrr!*'

'*Haaaaaaaaa!*'

'*Uuuuuuuuuuuuuuuuuooooooooooommmmmmmmmm!*'

'*Er-r-rk!*'

Mario, the bad king, who has just gasped his last, is

heaved out from behind the screen. With his legs and arms stretched out, he looks very dead. He smiles broadly when he comes off and everyone slaps him on the back and says how beautifully he carks it.

I am starting to feel a bit better. I wriggle an arm. I jingle.

'Shut up,' hisses Chook, 'I'm listening for my cue. If sound effects aren't made right on time it's bad news.' Then he starts making brisk clip-clopping sounds on coconut shells, for he hears his cue, which is, '"Did I hear the sound of hooves?"'

Everyone remembers their lines, comes in on cue and projects nicely. Lady Imogen and her ladies-in-waiting and the queens, even the bad one, look stunning with coloured scarves flowing from cone-shaped hats as they glide about the stage. Everybody's being theatrically brilliant. And Angie hasn't uttered one rude word.

The prompt could have packed up and gone home. He isn't needed. Not one person has to have their lines whispered to them from behind the trapdoor in front of the stage.

Sir is ecstatic. He's going bananas. He stops the rehearsal, because it's time for a break anyway, and he actually jumps up and down on the spot he's so happy. He's so off the planet he pulls a couple of ten-dollar notes out of his wallet and hands them out with orders to hotfoot it to Miss Peabody's to buy coke, twisties, chips . . . anything!

I stare at the waves of bodies charging for the door. I can't see *her*. I don't want to see her. Ever again. But there she is, with a gaggle of girls, all done up to look as like her as they possibly can. You wouldn't see as many curls at a hairdresser's. The girls think they're cool because they're like *her*. Pathetic dummies, all of them.

I'm just about to take off for Miss Peabody's, too, when I notice someone sitting on their own at the back of the hall. Glasses, and fair hair straight as a ruler. 'Who's that?' I ask Chook.

'That's the new girl. She's in Brown's class, but they're all on camp.'

'What's her name?'

'Lizzie.'

It might be just because I'm angry and hurt, but I straightaway think that, compared to the dummies fawning around Miss Joan, this girl really *is* cool.

To get out of the hall, I have to pass Miss Effington-Smythe and her admirers. I can feel her eyes on me. 'You look very handsome, Thomas,' she gushes.

Don't look. Don't turn. I do.

She's smiling. I want to smile back. I won't.

I do.

Kicking a chair on the way out of the hall makes me feel better.

I join the others making for Miss Peabody's. In our excellent costumes, we look as though we're off for a morning at a medieval tournament. An old lady hangs over her fence and waves.

Eventually, stocked up with chips courtesy of Sir, I come back to the hall. Again, there's the new girl, still sitting alone. I angle my way past her. I stop. I say, 'It's pretty pathetic, isn't it?'

She looks up. She's just like the little flower fairy in my *Flower Fairies of the Autumn* book that I got in kindy for being a well-behaved boy. Apart from the glasses.

'Everyone's happy, that's the important thing,' she says. And smiles.

She's the March fairy.

Sir's voice calls, 'Places, everyone.'

We're ready to start up again.

I give Lizzie a wave, nonchalant-like, and jingle towards the stage.

Foxy's arm muscles ripple as the curtains slide back to reveal the Lady Imogen with her hand to her brow. Chook's choir chants a very sorrowful *'Ahhhh!'* The bad knights, headed by Weasel, storm the castle to the sound of coconut shells being clapped together madly. Then everybody concentrates because it is at this moment that the drawbridge is to be lowered and so far this has been a disaster every time. But this time it sails down like a dream. Mad-Dog yells, 'You beauty!' but he can't be heard over the deafening coconut *clip-clops*. Then there is silence, because the bad knights are at the now vertical portcullis waiting to hear the words, '"The one whom you seek is amongst us."' That is the cue for the portcullis to rise. I glance left, watch it swing up gracefully and the bad knights, led by Weasel, charge through.

At this point I should confess that I haven't been doing much glancing to the left. I've been concentrating on a March fairy through the chink in the curtain.

We are reaching the climax of the play and Chook and his choir get ready for the big sword fight between the good knight and the bad knight. The cue comes from The Brain who declares, '"I have you in my power. You cannot escape."' Then the lunging and thrusting is on and Chook and his mob go ballistic with sound effects.

'Erggg!'

'Uuuuuuuuuuuuuuuuuu!'

'Eeee-rrr-ggggg!'

'Uuuuuuuuuuuuuuuuuuuuuuuuuu!'

'Aahhhh aaahhhhhh aaaahhhhhhhhhhhh!'

'Ergg!'

'Eggggg!'

'Uuuuuuuuuuuuuuuuuuuuuuuuuuuuuuuuuuuuuuuuuuuuuuuuuuuu!'

Now the bad knight is dead and it's time for others to drag him off the stage and for me to deliver my line. However, my eye is glued to the chink in the curtain, and I'm more interested in what is in the audience than in The Brain brandishing his sword and preparing to give me my cue.

'"The moment, at last, is come,"' he announces.

Silence.

And then comes a different voice. And it is not the voice of the prompt, who has obviously fallen asleep from boredom.

No, it is the voice of Miss Joan Effington-Smythe. 'Reveal yourself, Thomas!' she calls from the back of the hall.

'Drop ya daks, ya nerd,' hisses a voice from behind the curtain.

I leap up. I charge onto the stage.

Help! I have a line. I know I have a line. But what is it?

The Brain is about to save me. '"The moment at last is come,"' he announces once more.

'"Reveal yourself and flee."'

'More sparkle, Thomas.' It's *her* again. It's her voice floating from the back of the hall. 'This is a very important line. The whole play hinges on it.'

It does?

I think I'm going to throw up.

Something Wonderful

Grandma lives on the other side of town. Her unit is on the river, which winds through the suburbs. A river is a very pleasant thing to watch when you're following it in a bus.

Weed and I stare from the window and I rehearse what I'm going to say to Grandma about my father. I practise on Weed. But Weed stops me almost before I've begun.

'It'd be better to tell her about someone else, like Mad-Dog's dad, or just a friend's dad,' he explains. 'Then, when Grandma's all worked up, you say to her, "By the way, it's actually your own son we're talking about. My dad."'

Where would I be without my best buddy?

Now, my grandma is as famous for her homemade sausage rolls as she is for her strawberry layer cake. Today she has made both. And to be eating both is a very nice start to the visit.

Grandma's yakking on about how excellent school was in her day. And, while Weed is stuffing his face, he gives me a look that says, 'Hurry up and get on with it.'

'We're gonna ask you something, Gran. To get your opinion.'

'Yes, Pet?'

I stop. I look at Grandma's hands. Grandma's plate-sized hands. I imagine one rolled into a fist and connecting with my father's jaw. I'm thinking that a broken jaw is not great advertising for a barrister. So I say, 'I've forgotten.'

'You don't concentrate, Pet. Reed concentrates, don't you Reed?'

'Yes.'

'Yes what?'

'Yes, Grandma.'

'So, what's this all about?'

'Well—' says Weed.

'Out with it, Reed.'

Weed starts up. 'We have a friend, and he's sad and unhappy and wants to die—'

'Speak up, Reed.'

'He wants to die because his dad's about to run off with some other lady who's not my friend's mum. And his dad is never coming back.'

'Your friend should tell him "Good Riddance". What does he want for a father, a man or a mouse?'

Weed gulps. 'But our friend wants his dad. He wants him real bad.'

'He can look for another one if he's that desperate. There's plenty around.'

This is not what she's supposed to say. This is all wrong.

I butt in. 'We could be talking about my dad—'

Grandma turns to me. 'Who'd have *him*? He's such a grump.'

Weed gabbles on. 'Our friend's mum is sad and unhappy and wants to die too.'

'Tell her not to be a weakling and that she's better off without him. Tell her to take up karate if she thinks she needs protection.' Grandma gets up from her chair. 'Right, Reed?'

'Er, yes.'

'Yes what?'

'Yes, Grandma. Thank you, Grandma.'

'I have something wonderful for you that you'll find very interesting, Pet,' Grandma says to me. 'You will too, Reed. Wait there.'

She leaves the room and returns with a small box. She sets it on the table, and, with great ceremony, lifts the lid.

I stare. I don't know what they are. Weed stares. He shoots me a look. He hasn't a clue what they are either.

'I bought them for your play, Pet. I want to be able to hear every word you say. With these.'

It turns out that *these* are hearing aids. I thought they were something that had fallen out of the back of the TV.

'Very nice,' says Weed.

'Very nice? Very nice?'

'They're very nice, Grandma.'

There is another parcel on the table.

'Happy Birthday for the tenth of the month, Pet.'

It's the *Complete Works of Shakespeare*.

'To go with the lovely theatre,' Gran crows. 'Would you like me to quote some lines from Hamlet?'

We stand at the bus stop and watch the river go by. This was not what I had expected at all. I expected Grandma to be sympathetic to Mad-Dog's plight and to tell us how to help him. And then I expected to guide the conversation to my own plight, and Grandma was supposed to be even more sympathetic ... and also very cooperative and helpful in getting my parents back together. But instead it would appear that Gran doesn't think much of men. And she particularly doesn't seem to think much of her own son. Which makes me think that if my father had been there at Gran's, he would have studied the facts and drawn conclusions, and these conclusions would have made him very grumpy indeed.

I look down at Weed. His expression is grumpy, also.

'There's nothing else for it,' he announces. 'It's time for desperate measures.'

'Like what?'

'You've gotta be kidnapped,' he says.

I'm about to ask him what on earth he's going on about, but I decide I've had enough facts to study for one afternoon.

Greasepaint

We pile into the hall and make our way backstage to the men's dressing room. Today's rehearsal is about make-up. Or, as they say in the theatre, greasepaint.

In comes Sir. He's carrying a large box and a small book. He places the box on the table and invites us to gather around. He gives a well-projected cough and picks up the small book, which is a book of instructions that was, by the look of it, written in about 1066, and he starts to read.

'The following are essential: a good mirror, at least three 100-watt globes, removal cream.'

'For removing what, Sir?' asks Mario.

'Patience, my boy.' Sir continues to read. 'Cotton wool, spirit gum, some old towels, face powder, a powder puff, black mascara—'

'Can we keep what we don't use?' asks Angie.

'This is school property, Angelica.'

'Bum.'

'Orange sticks—'

'You can get those at Miss Peabody's, Sir.'

'Not this kind of orange stick, you can't.'

Sir opens the box and pulls out a bright orange stick. 'Leichners, the best,' he reads off the label. 'Used by Edmund Kean almost two hundred years ago.'

It smells like it. There is a lot of heavy coughing.

Sir reads on. 'Straight make-up for men. Greasepaint number five.'

He breaks off and says, 'I will demonstrate. Any volunteers?'

'Me, Sir,' pipes up Spud.

Spud O'Toole is a redhead. His face is red, too. In fact everything about him is red. So I suppose that he thinks a change of colour would be a good idea.

Spud goes up to the table.

'Now,' says Sir, adjusting his glasses and peering at the book. 'One. Make sure the face is clean. Two. Grease the face with removal cream. Close your eyes.' Sir begins to slap on dollops of cream.

'Ouch.'

'Good. Now we know that the make-up we use will come off easily. Three. Apply a number five stick in rough streaks over the face and neck, and rub it in.' Sir does so and stands back to look at the effect. 'If you have applied too much the result will look porridgy.' We examine the face and indeed it does look rather porridgy.

'Ouch! It's going up my nose.'

Much laughing from the rest of us.

'Four. Draw a short streak of number nine greasepaint under each cheekbone and repeat this with a carmine two. The cheek colour makes the face look alive.' We all peer at

Spud to see if his face looks alive. And believe it or not, it not only looks alive but also quite excellent.

'Five. The eyes … Now six, lightly pencil in the eyebrows … seven, mascara, eight, powder lightly …'

There are loud coughing noises and flapping hands.

Spud is so enthusiastic about how excellent he looks that when Sir suggests that he turns Spud into an old man, Spud says yes. We've all watched Laurence Olivier turning into old King Lear on the DVD that Sir showed us. And now Spud wants to do the same.

Sir goes about shading and highlighting and wrinkling and purpling and greying, and soon Spud looks ancient, although with his front tooth coloured black, he also looks like a thug.

Now Sir thinks he's genius material and he gets more ambitious. 'Would you like a nose?' he asks Spud.

This seems a strange question. Spud already has a nose.

'Eighteen. Nose putty. To build up the nose—'

The Brain seems to be thinking that it would be wiser to have the removal cream directly under the nose, rather than layers of make-up, if he ever wants to get it off again.

'Shouldn't that have gone on first, Sir?' The Brain asks.

But Sir has already stuck on the putty and is moulding it into an enormous nose shape.

'We can chisel it off later.'

'Ow!' squeaks Spud in anticipation.

'Nineteen. The Hair. A: artificial hair. B: hair powder.'

Sir has finally come to the end of the book. A black-bearded, black-haired, large-nosed, elderly Spud turns to us and bows. We applaud, still coughing from the black powder.

Now it is our turn. And I am to make up Harry Falk, who is also a guard. And who would like to be a hairy guard because he has very little hair, even on his eyebrows.

Soon Harry has multicoloured snakes wriggling over his face and he has rather a lot of hair growing from his cheeks and forehead. The spirit gum has gone everywhere, including all over my fingers, which are now stuck together.

Sir is doing the rounds, admiring our creative genius. He comes to me and remarks that I have created an unusually hairy guard. But he adds that luckily it will all come off very easily with the removal cream. Which I have forgotten to use.

I won't go on about what happens next.

To Dye, to Sleep No More

It's Tuesday morning, I'm making my way to the classroom and Mad-Dog is talking to me about Spud.

'Spud's green,' he tells me. And he says it with only a twitch of a smile.

'What?'

'He's turned green.'

'How green?'

'Real green.'

'All over green?'

'Just his hair.'

'He dyed it?' I say, thinking of Spud's mum.

Now, one of the things I know about Spud is that his mum's hair is black, but that it's dyed that way. I know this because his mum is the dental nurse at the clinic where we go. One day, as she bent to adjust the paper serviette under my chin, I noticed that she had a line of grey hair on top. So Spud has most likely seen his mum's hair turning from grey to black, and apparently he has now decided to do something similar.

Mad-Dog lives next door to Spud, and Mad-Dog tells

me that Spud asked him to help him do the back of his head. A thing that it is very difficult to do for yourself unless you are an owl.

'Yeah.'

'Why didn't he dye it black? He was going ape about having black hair when Sir did his make-up.'

'He did go black. Till he got out in the sun. Then his hair started to go green. Nice, though. Sort of grass colour.'

'Can't you wash it out?'

'Nup. Semi-permanent.'

'Well semi-permanent's not real permanent. Why didn't he dye it back?'

'He says he's never gonna touch a bottle of dye again as long as he lives.'

'I bet.'

'It's a nice sort of green. The guards could all do it,' says Mad-Dog, experiencing a flash of genius. 'Dye their hair green. The Guards of the Green Hair. Like The Knights of the Round Table.'

'Not a good idea. I'm a guard.'

'So? I reckon it'd be cool.'

We look around for Spud. By now everybody has heard about his hair, and others are looking around for him too. We finally spot him sitting on a step looking sad, with a woollen beanie pulled down to his eyebrows. Mad-Dog suggests he take it off as everyone is keen to have a look. But Spud pulls the beanie lower and shakes his head. A couple of hands lunge at his beanie and miss, and now Spud's whole body, as well as his head, is shaking.

Unexpectedly, it's The Brain who comes up with a

solution. He peers at Spud closely and says, '"To die: to sleep; no more."'

'What?'

'Sir Laurence Olivier went blond once. He bleached his hair to play Hamlet. Do you think he liked it? Think of lying awake night after night with bleached blond hair. But he always said, "What I do, I do for Art." As you have done, Spud. And we are proud of you.'

Everybody applauds wildly. And Spud stands up. He flings off his beanie and laughs. We laugh, too, because green hair really is something to laugh about.

Spud is convinced that he's now in the Laurence Olivier class.

And I'm thinking that he is too.

I'm thinking also of what Weed said when we were coming home from Grandma's. About desperate measures and kidnapping. Weed has been very secretive about his kidnapping plan. But he says he will reveal all after school today.

He also says that this is a plan that, unlike all the others so far, will actually work.

Desperate Measures

We are sitting under a tree in Weed's garden—Weed, Bugs and me. And Weed is telling Bugs about the plan we'll be putting into operation in a couple of hours time.

'Kidnapping is desperate measures,' declares Weed.

'Kidnapping who?' asks Bugs.

'Me,' I say.

'For money?'

'Nuh.'

'What's the use of being kidnapped if you don't score a heap of cash?'

It is obvious that Bugs watches a lot of television.

We continue to explain the plan to Bugs.

'What we want is my mum and dad to be together again. And Weed reckons that a big-time worry about something important to them both would make this happen.'

'Like what?'

'Like me. When I don't come home from school they will get together to worry. Because when you don't come home from school, it's obvious you've been kidnapped.'

'Where will you be?'

'In the shed.'

'What shed?'

'My shed,' says Weed. 'Six o'clock will come and there'll be no Tom at Tom's house, and Tom's mum will start to worry. She'll ring you, Bugs, and ask, "Do you know where he is?"'

'And I tell her he's in the shed?'

'You say that you do not know. The last time you saw him was in class.'

'Okay.'

'Then she rings here. Same answer. Get it?'

'Yeah.'

'Then she rings the school, and asks is there a rehearsal? There is no rehearsal. She rings Mad-Dog's, she rings everyone she can think of. It's getting dark. She's frantic. She rings *him*. He charges around. He holds her hand. He tells her of all the big-time criminals he's cornered and promises that he will find their ever-loving son.'

'And will he?'

Weed gives Bugs a withering look. 'So, now,' he goes on, 'we prepare Tom a very nice dinner of sandwiches and bring him blankets, and in he goes.'

'Where?'

'Into the shed.'

'Does he have to stay all night in the shed?'

'Yeah.'

'Right till morning?'

'Yeah.'

At this point, I'm thinking that while this sounds

like an excellent plan, I'd rather it was happening to someone else.

Weed says to Bugs, 'You go home. I'll go inside. And
we wait.'

'What for?'

'For the phone calls, which will come soon after six.'

'Three problems,' says Bugs, who has been around Weed
for long enough to sometimes think laterally himself. 'One.
Why can't he just walk out when he gets sick of being in
the shed? Two. When his mum and dad find out what
we've done, that's what they'll want to know, too. Three.
The cops, who'll be spending a lot of time looking down
drains and up trees, will not be very happy when they find
out it was a trick. And they *will* find out.' He stops, then
adds, 'Like on *The Bill*.'

Weed sighs. 'When people are locked in, they can't get
out unless they have a key. And there's only one key and it
hangs on a nail outside the door. So . . .'

But Bugs goes on. 'The cops'll be nosing around here.
Because they know that in every murder mystery, the
garden shed is where you are likely to find the body. And
when they find Tom in there, they'll want to know who
locked him in and why.'

'He's been locked in *accidentally*, of course,' replies Weed.
'He went into the shed to get . . . er . . . What did you go
into the shed for, Tom?'

'Er . . . methylated spirits.'

'Why methylated spirits?'

'Got a mark on my jeans.'

'Then,' Weed continues, 'I say that I came by, saw that

the door to the shed was wide open, took the key and locked it.'

'What's accidental about that?'

'We are setting up a situation, Bugs. It's called being imaginative.'

I say nothing. Weed's garden shed is a very dark place. And a cold one. I am also wondering whether certain mums and dads wouldn't be quite happy to be rid of a son who doesn't clean up his room, and whether these desperate measures are going to work.

'Where's your mum through all of this, Weed?' asks Bugs.

'She doesn't get home till six.' Weed looks at his watch. 'Which is in five minutes.'

Now Bugs goes home so his mum doesn't start to think *he's* been kidnapped. And Weed and I head for the shed. Weed tells me to have a very long pee, as I will be here for a very long time. He goes into the house and returns with an armful of blankets and something wrapped in Christmas paper.

'Bean sprouts,' he says. 'For vitamins and minerals.'

'I thought I was having sandwiches.'

'You'll need vitamins and minerals,' nods Weed wisely. He now takes from its nail a small silver key.

He pushes me in, gives me a wave, locks the door and off he goes. And I am stuck in the garden shed with a mountain of bean sprouts. And the night closing in.

I would rather be anywhere else.

I glance around. A spider is crawling along the floor towards me. Then comes the scurry of little feet. Mice feet. I draw the blankets tighter. A cockroach is creeping up the blanket. From somewhere comes a *tap-tap-tapping*. The branch of a tree, on the tiny window, is going *tap tap tap*. I pull the blankets higher. I'm scared. And it's going to be *all night*.

I try to concentrate on things that are safe and warm and mouse-less. I think about home and what is supposed to be happening there.

I later find out that what's happening is this:

At 4.15 my mum sits down at the kitchen table and writes me a note. The note tells me that she is off to meet up with an old school chum, after which she'll be going to the school for a committee meeting. My dinner's in the microwave. And she won't be home till nine. She puts the note on the sugar bin. And leaves.

It is now 8.45 and very dark and very cold. And I'm thinking that by now even furry animals and baby birds are tucked up in their little holes and nests, feeling warm and cosy. Bugs is probably stretched out by a nice warm fire, watching his favourite program. Weed will be stretched out on his bed reading his favourite book. Weed's mum'll be making her poppyseed bread.

And unbeknownst to me, my mum is only just on her way home.

But on her way home she passes Weed's house. And suddenly she remembers the gardening books that Weed's mum says she will lend her to help her with her herb garden.

So she stops.

Weed's mum says she's left the books in the shed. She picks up the torch. She won't be a minute she says, and, with light bobbing, she leaves my mum in the kitchen and off she goes.

She takes the small silver key off the nail, opens the door, sees someone lying on the floor of the shed and screams very loudly. Hollers and bangs for someone to come. My mother, who is at the back door of the house, starts to grope her way through the dark . . .

I say. 'It's me.'

'It's who?'

I throw off the blankets and stand. 'It's Tom.'

Weed's mum's hand is shaking so much the light's wobbling.

'You sound like Tom!'

'I am Tom.'

I clump back to the house in the wake of Weed's mum and the wobbling torchlight.

'What are you doing here at this time of night?' Mum barks. And to Weed's mum, 'What is he doing here?'

'Haven't a clue. Tom?'

I've had enough. I'm cold. I'm tired. I've eaten a mountain of bean sprouts and I feel sick. I am sick. I'm sick of everything. I'm sick of moronic plays. I'm sick of plans that keep failing. I'm sick of blondes who keep scheming. I'm sick of grandmas who keep stalling. I'm sick of Dad.

'I don't feel very well,' I mutter.

I sit in the back seat of the car.

'What was all that about?' my mother asks as she pulls into the road. 'And where, through all of this, was Weed?'

Good question. Where were Weed and his lateral thinking when I needed them?

'You don't know anything,' I mutter.

'Then tell me.'

There's too much to explain, and right now I don't care any more. I'm fed up with Weed and his stupid desperate measures, and all the stupid fail-proof plans that have failed every stupid time. I'm so fed up, I'm yelling, 'If you want to know, ask *him*! Ask your husband!'

'What in the world has he got to do with you being locked in Weed's mother's shed?'

I start to cry.

My mother drives on.

Full Dress Rehearsal

I'm woken this morning by the phone. It's Weed. He's acting like last night was no big deal. He reckons if you saw that sort of thing on the telly you'd think it was funny. I tell him that he wasn't the one who was locked up. I go on to remind him that he also wasn't the one who had to front up to two irate mothers when I was dragged out of the shed.

In the kitchen my mother is making toast. Did she ring Dad, I wonder? She might have rung him last night after I went to bed. I went straight to bed without saying anything, so she might have . . .

But I don't ask. I don't want to know.

What *she* wants to know is did I have a nice sleep; then, 'I want a word with you,' she says.

Time to go. It's definitely time to go.

Weed once told me his mum says that worrying about two things at the same time is an excellent strategy for a nervous breakdown. So I am refusing to think about last night or about anything to do with it, because *this* night it is Full Dress Rehearsal. Which is in itself a Big-time Worry.

I ooze my way through the day. School finishes. I go

home. I eat a strand of spaghetti. Mum drives me back to school.

By seven o'clock everybody is assembled on the stage. In the hall, seats are now lined up in rows.

Sir is standing in the aisle. He calls for silence. He tells us that Brown's class will be coming to watch the rehearsal. He also announces that Miss Effington-Smythe will be late.

I know why. I know where she is. It's Wednesday.

Anyway, I'm relieved. I don't want to see that smile again. Especially when it's smiled at me. It still hurts too much, believe it or not.

Sir invites us all to *break a leg*. You never say 'good luck' in the theatre, especially not on opening night, because it actually means *bad* luck. If you do say it, you're asking for trouble. So now we are telling everyone very nicely to break a leg. And while this is usually only said on actual performance nights, Sir has suggested that, as tonight could be called a first performance, it is appropriate for us to practise saying it.

There is a lot of heavy activity backstage with people pulling on costumes and passing orange sticks and grease-paint around. And Jenny is winding me into my chain mail and sticking it together with the Velcro she's bought, which means I can slip in and out of my costume easily. And everyone is considering breaking a leg, which means acting the professional. Guards are projecting and breathing from the diaphragm, ladies and ladies-in-waiting are lowering themselves in and out of chairs, good and bad kings are walking around with books on their heads, and knights are bending very beautifully to pick up their swords.

Around me there's a quiet confidence. And when some nerd yells, 'Two more sleeps', there's nodding and smiling because everyone is anticipating being professional on *the night*.

Spud jangles his way towards me and I stare at him in amazement. He looks super cool. He has shaved all the green hair off his head. And now there are just tiny little spikes of red hair popping up all over it. And very proud of them he is. And that makes everybody laugh and slap him on the back.

And every now and then I wonder, will the flower fairy be coming? It's not compulsory ...

I peer through the chink in the curtain. Mr Brown's class has arrived. A couple of other teachers have come along too. The kids all slink into seats. But I don't see her. She's not coming.

Yes she is! She's there! Glasses and hair straight as a ruler. She's with Amy whats-her-name who's on crutches. She holds a crutch while Amy sits.

I must blank out everything. The home front. Everything. I must concentrate.

At 7.58 Foxy starts flexing his curtain-pulling muscles, because we are told that if you're going to be professional, you have to start on time.

We are all ready.

Sir is neither standing nor pacing. He is sitting. Which shows he's quietly confident, too. On the dot of eight o'clock the curtains slide back and on strides Weasel, rattling his plastic rings. And we're off.

But this time we're off to not-a-very-good start because

Weasel has accidentally pierced Lady Imogen's cone-shaped hat and veil with his sword. It is now ripped in two and the Lady Imogen is yanking at it angrily, saying very unLady-Imogen-like words. The veil is completely shredded and she is so cross she jumps up and down on it.

This results in lots of giggling from the audience, followed by a hissed, 'Outside if you're going to laugh,' from one of the teachers.

Back on stage, Lady Imogen is snarling at The Brain because, not only has she lost her flowing headgear but he is hiccupping at her. He has been sipping water like Laurence Olivier. But he has been doing it too quickly.

'"I ... *hic* ... see a far-off ... *hic* ... *hic* ... *hic* ... castle ... *hic* ... with a ... *hic* ... moat ... and a ... *hic* ... port ... *hic* ... cullis ..."'

'Oh God!' This is not in the script, but the Lady Imogen has a lot of time to say things between *hics* that the play-wright hadn't thought of. Then Mario, who is the bad king, notices something different about the stage. He sees that there are two spy screens hanging up, when there should only be one, because big-time artist Nigel couldn't make up his mind which of the two he designed was the more beautiful. So he has decided to sneak both onto the stage, which now presents a problem, because the bad king doesn't know which screen to hide behind to get knifed in the gut. And he chooses the wrong one.

So when The Brain comes on and hiccups, '"Dead ... *hic* ... for a duc ... *hic* ... at ... dead,"' and plunges his sword into the screen on the right, a voice from behind the one on the left moans, '"Oh, I am slain!"' This presents a problem, as it would be impossible for anyone to be slain from a position on the other side of the stage, unless the murderer had a twenty-metre sword.

'Stop!' wails Sir.

But the good knight is hiccupping on. Behind the scenes, Chook and his choir are madly searching for the box of coconut shells, which seem to have gone missing.

'Who's got the coconut shells?'

'"What is that c ... *hic* ... c ... *hic* ... castle nearby ... *hic*?"'

'Some jerk's stolen the coconut shells!'

'Hey, Sir! We can't find the coconut shells.'

But there is no reply. Sir is slumped in his chair.

A teacher in the audience hisses 'Shh!!' again at someone in Brown's class.

'"Did I hear the sound of hooves?"' projects the good king.

Silence.

'"Did I hear the sound of hooves?"'

Silence.

'I should have flaming-well heard the sound of flaming hooves!'

'*Clip, clop, clip, clop,*' chant Chook's sound effects team, sounding very un-hoof-like.

The bad knights, led by Weasel, rush to the drawbridge, which should now be coming down. But Mad-Dog has redesigned the pulling system with a spring, so that the drawbridge can swing up and down smoothly. However, a drawbridge is supposed to stay down long enough for bad knights to clip-clop across. And this one keeps springing up and down and up and down before they can get a foot on it. So the knights are forced to march around and around the stage while Mad-Dog tries to make the drawbridge stay down.

Since there is not even a murmur from the director's chair we push on. And off, in the case of Lady Imogen, who, by this time, is showing her teeth.

'"C . . . *hic* . . . come . . . *hic* . . . my d . . . *hic* . . . d . . . *hic* . . . dear . . ."'

'God!' Lady Imogen kicks at her veil, which is still floating in pieces on the floor, then storms off the stage and marches straight through the audience to the door, colliding, as she leaves, with Miss Effington-Smythe who has just entered the hall. And who is now prostrate on the floor.

Actors charge off the stage and race towards her.

'Hey!' screams the stage manager, who is supposed to manage such things. 'Come back!'

But it is too late. Half the cast, as well as the backstage crew, are at the door helping Miss Effington-Smythe to her feet. Meanwhile, the Lady Imogen has left. Not only left the stage and the hall, but left the school. With her lacy gown billowing out behind her, she is screaming into her mobile phone for a parent to come and take her home.

'Back!' shrieks the stage manager.

Everyone charges back, amid the cheers of Mr Brown's class.

The teachers hiss again for them to be quiet.

The drama has awakened Sir, who is now supporting Miss Effington-Smythe's head to stop the nosebleed.

On stage, The Brain is looking rather pale, but he

remembers Laurence Olivier and hiccups on. '"I ... *hic* ... have you in my ... *hic* ... *hic* ... *hic* ... power. You cannot ... *hic* ... escape."'

He lunges at Weasel with his sword. And as he does he trips over the remains of Lady Imogen's cone-shaped hat which is poking out from the edge of the prompt box. With a curse he lets go of his sword and it sails down into the prompt box, connecting with the left ear of Spin Bowler, who is the prompt. There is a loud howl of pain and some very original expressions. But these expressions are drowned out by Chook and his team who are still making sword-fighting noises even though there's no one left fighting.

'*Erggg!*'

'*Uuuuuuuuuuuuuuuuuuuuuuuuuuuuuuuuuu!*'

'*Eee rrr ggggg!*'

'*Uuuuuuuuuuuuuuuuuuuuuuuuuuuuuuuuuuuuuuuuuuuuuuu!*'

'Oh, SHUT UP!' bellows the still-very-alive bad king.

Matthew Wigg, who is the good king, tries to haul Spin Bowler out of the prompt box but he loses his balance and falls headfirst into the prompt box himself. We've learnt in sport that to fall in this manner is not a good idea. Not even if you are rescuing your best buddy.

The good king is calling for a bucket, saying he's broken his foot and that he is going to be sick.

But suddenly I hear, '"The moment ... *hic hic* ... at last ... *hic* ... *hic* ..."'

That is my cue. Which means it is now time for me to say my line. I am shaking. My heart is crashing around in my ears again.

On I go. I must project with fire and passion. I wait and I wait for The Brain to finish his line.

'"... *hic* ... is come."'

I open my mouth wide ...

'"Relieve yourself and fleeeeee."'

Silence.

'No!' It's Sir's voice.

'No what?'

'That was wrong, Thomas.' This time it is *her* voice.

'What was wrong?'

'What you said.'

'I said, "Reveal yourself and flee".'

'No, you didn't.'

Oh no. I've heard this before. Help, help, help!

'What did I say?'

Please, please, please, please, please, don't let me have said ...

'You said, "Relieve yourself and flee."'

I suddenly feel unwell.

There is a long silence. Partly because the Lady Imogen is supposed to come on again to say her last lines, and she is not there.

More sniggers from the audience, and more stern hushing noises.

'Someone stand in!' orders the stage manager.

Spud steps forward. When you're that confident about the way your hair looks, you're inclined to do anything.

He minces up to The Brain. 'Yes, darling?'

'Oh ... *hic* ... *hic* ... *hic* ... God!'

The curtains close. There is silence except for the sounds

of moaning and throwing up from inside the prompt box.

'A ... *hic* ... *hic* ... bad rehear ... *hic* ... sal means a ... *hic* ... *hic* ... *hic* ... good performance ... *hic*. That's what ... *hic* ... Laur ... *hic* ... Laur ... *hic* ... Laurence Olivi—'

We turn to The Brain as one.

'Oh, *shut up*!'

Panic
Stations

I *am* having a nervous breakdown. (*Reveal, reveal, reveal, reveal, reveal, reveal.*)

I have only two more days and one more sleep to get over it. That, and to stop shaking, sweating, stuttering (*r-r-reveal, r-r-reveal, r-r-reveal*) and throwing up.

The nightmare is back. Shakespeare is right—"'To die: to sleep; no more.'" I am dying. I am sleeping no more . . .

(*Reveal, reveal, reveal.*)

I've got two days and one sleep to turn from jellyfish to sturdy guard . . .

(*Reveal, reveal, reveal.*)

I shake and stutter my way through classes. (*Reveal, reveal, reveal.*) I am not happy. I am anxious. I look at everybody else. They also look unhappy. And anxious. It's very difficult to be a hundred percent cooperative when you are unhappy and anxious. And it doesn't help at all to know that your prompt (who you rely on with your life) has an infected ear as the result of a flying sword. (*Reveal, reveal, reveal.*) And that Matthew Wigg is now a good king on crutches. (*Reveal, reveal, reveal.*)

I can't think about my father. I can't think about him or the Blonde One or anyone else till after Friday. I just can't.

It is Thursday. And in another sixteen hours it will be Friday (*reveal, reveal, reveal*). And then at eight pm on the dot ... (*Reveal, reveal, reveal.*)

My mother has come home from her hairdresser in the city, who, like all city hairdressers, can be very imaginative when he is allowed to be. It's hard to describe the hair-do (*reveal, reveal, reveal*), except that it looks like a mountain with waterfalls of grey that flow from a pinnacle of snow. Her hair, which is long to start with, rises up and up.

(*Reveal, reveal, reveal.*)

'Does it meet with approval?' she asks. 'I said to Trevor, "Tomorrow is a night of great pith and moment. Be creative. I must be seen."'

It strikes me that while she will certainly be seen, anyone sitting behind her will be seeing nothing. (*Reveal, reveal, reveal.*)

'I am the mother of an *artiste*,' she's chirruping.

(*Reveal, reveal, reveal.*)

'They're all coming,' she sparkles, keeping her head steady. 'Grandma and Myrtle and—'

'I gotta go.'

'Wait!' My mother has suddenly stopped sparkling. 'Tom, sit down. There's something I've got to tell you. Something that you need to know ...'

No, no! No more!

I clap my hands over my ears like I used to do when I was little. 'I can't hear you!' And I stagger off to the loo.

(*Reveal, reveal, reveal, reveal, reveal, reveal.*)

I sit there shaking. Gloop follows me in. He looks concerned. And sad.

I start to think. And I think to myself, what if I get sick? What if I succumb to a strange and exotic illness overnight? I have symptoms enough for anything. Then I think back to the first full rehearsal and remember how excellent it was. I remember Sir jumping up and down with happiness and pulling ten-dollar notes out of his pockets for us to buy anything we wanted. I think of how proud *we* all were, too. I think of Mad-Dog slaving away day and night to make the drawbridge work and Nigel painting not one spy screen, but two, so we would have the very best. I think of Chook's team and their magnificent sound effects with coconuts, and of Spud dyeing his hair to lend a touch of elegance to the scene. I think of Spin Bowler, whose ear has become infected, of Matthew Wigg, who has sacrificed a foot, and Weasel, who lost a bit of his finger when his hand got caught in the portcullis. And The Brain trying to keep everybody positive through his hiccups ... And I think of us all watching DVDs of Laurence Olivier so that we'd be inspired to be excellent. And I am suddenly filled with a warm, fuzzy glow.

'If we did it once, we can do it again! Right, Gloop?'

Gloop studies me carefully. And sadly.

(*Reveal, reveal, reveal.*)

Grandma's Ears

And now the day is come. Which is odd, as, for the last six weeks, I have been confident that it never would, that the day would somehow be passed over, eclipsed, forgotten or simply left out of the calendar.

But the day has finally come. And with it, rain.

(*Reveal, reveal, reveal.*)

I walk home through rain which I hardly feel, even though the gutters are gushing like rivers, and there is a cold snake of water trickling down something that might once have been my back. (*Reveal, reveal, reveal.*) I walk because a person needs legs to ride a bike. Not things that feel like shaking rubber hoses.

I have deeply breathed my way through double maths (*reveal, reveal, reveal*), and watched everybody else doing the same. (*Reveal, reveal, reveal.*) And now we're all going straight home so that there'll be time to prepare for a really decent panic attack.

I sludge up to the front door to discover that Mum has also been walking in the rain. The magnificent hair-do has sunk into sad little strands clinging to her scalp and down the sides of her face.

'Oh, my God! Look at me! Just look at me . . .'

I can't. I can't.

I won't.

I feel sick. I limp to the loo. Perhaps a quiet sitting will revive at least a shred of the confidence I felt about a hundred and fifty years ago. (*Reveal, reveal, reveal.*) Then again, I just might remain here forever. I can see the head-lines: 'Boy's skeleton found after twenty years in disused loo.'

I am carefully considering this option when they all arrive. My father (with guard-like stance), Myrtle (with bowels), Ida (who's Grandma's buddy) and Grandma. They are all set to come to the play, except Dad who has turned up just to wish me luck and to announce that he's heading off straight after dinner to study notes for a session first thing in the morning.

When he first makes this announcement no one seems to be listening.

Grandma is wearing her brand new state-of-the-art hearing aids. Which, as you know, have been purchased at mind-blowing expense for the sole purpose of coming to the play and hearing every word of it. The problem is, she doesn't know how to work them properly yet. She keeps twiddling with them, which makes them either shriek or groan. And I am thinking how nice it would be if she could just disappear somewhere. (*Reveal, reveal, reveal.*) Because otherwise there'll be shrieking and groaning all through the play. (*Reveal, reveal, reveal.*)

Dinner comes and goes. Mine stays untouched. (*Reveal, reveal, reveal.*) I can see two of everything.

My father, having polished off his dessert as well as mine, gets up from the table. But before he leaves, he says, 'Goodbye.'

This prompts the following dialogue:

Grandma: Why are you saying good-bye when we're all going together?

Dad: Because we're not all going together.

Grandma: (turning up new, state-of-the-art hearing aids) (*iiiiiiiiiiiiiiiiiii*) What?

Dad: *We are not all going together!*

Myrtle: I know. It's me that's going in the Volvo. Me with you.

Dad: No. It's me that's going in the Volvo. Me without you.

Grandma: On your own? That's very selfish.

Me: I think I'm going to throw up.

Grandma: (turning down new, state-of-the-art hearing aids) (*uuuuuuuuuuuuuuuu*) Try deep breathing, Pet. In through the nose, and out through the mouth. In and out. In and out.

Dad: I'm sorry, Tom. It's this case . . .

Grandma: Come on, everyone. Everything into the dish-washer . . .

Myrtle: I'm going now.

Mum: Just wait a moment . . .

Myrtle: You know I can't wait. (Exits to the toilet)

Grandma: It's her bowels.

Dad: I'm off.

Grandma: (turning up new, state-of-the-art hearing aids) (*iiiiiiiiiiiiii*) He says he's not going!

Mum: Of course he's going.

Me: *Reveal, reveal, reveal.*

Dad: (moving towards door) I'll call you, Tom.

Grandma: You don't have to. You're right here.

Dad: I have a mediation tomorrow morning, first thing. I am going now.

Grandma: (positioning herself by door and turning down new, state-of-the-art hearing aids) (*иииииииииии*) Oh, no you're not.

Dad: Oh, yes I am.

Grandma: That boy has worked and studied and practised. Why? To give you pleasure.

Dad: Tom, is it important to you that I come?

Me: What?

Mum: As if you had to ask!

Myrtle: (re-entering) Now I feel better.

Mum: We'll have to take the Volvo. It's got the extra seat in the back.

Dad: The Volvo is *my* car.

Mum: We won't all fit in the Mazda. You can give the Mazda a nice long run on Sunday.

Dad: What's on Sunday?

Mum: The wedding.

Dad: What wedding?

Grandma: Who is having a wedding?

Mum: A barrister mate of your son's.

Dad: Oh, *that* wedding! Right, yes, that's miles away, in the country.

Mum: Don't *you* complain. The wedding's on because of you. (To Grandma) The girl's mum was killed in a car accident. The marriage was going to be postponed. But now she and what's-his-name . . .

Dad: Guy.

Mum: Now she and Guy are getting married on Sunday. Tom's dad talked her into going ahead with it. She was terribly upset, and he took her for coffee—

Dad: At that little place on the corner. The morning Tom and his friend were there.

Me: What?

Dad: It was a school day, too, I recall.

Me: What?

Mum: Her name's Kate. I haven't met her, but I'm sure I'll like her.

Dad: Tom likes Kate.

Me: What?

Dad: Tom and Kate had a nice little chat on the first floor of 461. Thursday, wasn't it, Tom? The day I was interstate.

Me: What?

Mum: That was *after* school. He didn't skip classes *that* day.

I don't believe it! Mum knows everything and Dad knows everything . . . They've twigged to what I've been up to. Which means they must also have twigged to the fact that I got it all wrong!

And now Mum's telling everyone how she rang Dad after I left for rehearsal that morning, and how she told Dad about me being locked in the shed, and how I said *she* should ask *him* about it. And now Mum's telling how Dad told her about the business in the cafe and how me and Weed fronted up to his apartment, and how I went to chambers and talked to Kate. And Mum's waving her arms around and saying how she had tried to explain it all to me, but that I had refused to listen . . .

Mum: And when I said to Tom's father that Tom should have been at school instead of hanging around in cafes, he said that Tom was showing a bit of spunk, and anyway, it was Tom's birthday . . .

Grandma: (turning up new, state-of-the-art hearing aids) (*iiiiiiiiiiii*) A minute ago you were talking about a wedding. Now you're talking about a birthday.

'I think I'm going to be sick,' I say. 'I really am.'

'Keep up the deep breathing, Pet,' pipes up Gran. 'Breathe in and out. In and out.'

'I'm sick. So sick I can't go. I can't—'

'It's stage fright,' declares Mum. 'It's quite normal.'

'I won't be missed. I've only got one line!'

'One line! The whole play hinges on it!' shrieks my mother.

'Tom,' says my father, 'you are feeling foolish, that's all. This will pass. Now stop being a wimp and get into the car.'

I lurch to the loo for the hundred-and-fiftieth time. I farewell Gloop who just walks sadly past me. I wobble to the car. I slump onto the seat. My father shoots me a look. 'It would appear that you think any dad is better than no dad,' he says. 'Even a stuffy old grumpy one.'

I'm shaking all over. So I guess he concludes it's a nod.

Break a Leg

I wobble towards backstage (*reveal, reveal, reveal*) and push open the stage door. What I can make out, with my semi-blurred vision, looks quite encouraging. Everybody is bustling about, examining hair-dos, arranging props, collecting make-up, fixing costumes, walking, sitting, bending, and picking up things from the floor. There's parading of cone-shaped hats, jingling from chain mail and bubble humming (in stage whispers) to the back wall.

In the centre of all this activity is Sir, dressed in black with a silver chain around his neck, which makes him look a very big-time-director indeed. Although he's a slightly pale one.

He's saying that if we can do it once, we can do it again. And everybody is agreeing and smiling nervously and brandishing their swords, or nodding their cone-shaped hats. There's Spin Bowler, with his ear bandaged up, flourishing his prompt script, and Matthew Wigg attacking the air with his left crutch. There's Spud, whose hair has continued to grow in tiny red spikes. Mad-Dog is yakking to Sir (who is turning paler) about the new pulley system for the drawbridge that he's invented, and which he will be trying out for the first time tonight.

It starts to feel as if everything's going to be all right. And very soon that feeling turns into a quiet confidence that is not quiet at all. We move on to warming-up exercises. (*Reveal, reveal, reveal.*) We bend and lunge and loosen up very professionally indeed.

The stage looks like a magnificent scene from King Arthur's time, with Nigel's single but decorative spy screen, the straight-as-a-dye new portcullis, the colourful little sea creatures relaxing in the moat, the drawbridge with its sturdy chains, and the very lovely turrets and covered walkways. Behind the curtain, Chook's boxes of sound-effects equipment have been found and are all lined up in order and nailed securely to the floor.

Everybody and everything looks straight out of a twelfth-century magazine. The Lady Imogen (in her new headgear) and her ladies-in-waiting are floating around with their scarves flowing from their cone-shaped hats and putting their hands to their brows. Knights (both good and bad) with shining swords are lunging and thrusting and parrying. People are milling about with greasepaint and orange sticks and calling for black liners and blue, and hair powder and carmine two and being transformed into magnificent knights and kings and queens. Some are taking tiny sips of water like Laurence Olivier.

Now Jenny has finished stitching up the good queen's hem and is about to wind me into my chain mail. But first she hurries off to get the Velcro. Then she hurries back. 'I've left it at home,' she says. Again she hurries off and returns with needle and thread. 'You'll have to be sewn in.' For the next three-quarters of an hour (*reveal, reveal, reveal*) I am sewn into my chain mail. And a very good job she does too. She tucks, folds and pleats so well that it looks as though the costume might have been made for me.

And now (*reveal, reveal, reveal*) I draw breath to rehearse my line out loud, as this is what everybody else is doing. But nothing comes out. Not even a squeak. My vocal cords have gone into spasm. Panic! No. Sip a little water. That's it. That's what everybody's doing. That's what Laurence Olivier does. That's what the would-be-big-time-professional (alias my mother) advised many times before I wobbled in. 'Keep a glass of water handy to sip if your throat feels dry,' she warbled. 'All actors need their little sip.' I take a sip from one of the jugs of water that are standing around.

'Reveal yourself and f—' *Squeak.*

I sip again. 'Reveal yourself and f—' *Squeak.*

And again. 'Reveal yourself and fl—' *Squeak.*

I take a large gulp. 'Reveal yourself and flee.'

Got it.

Someone bellows, 'Fifteen minutes!' It's the stage manager, looking very efficient indeed. (*Reveal, reveal, reveal.*)

'Reveal yourself and flee.' Another gulp.

'Reveal yourself and fleeeee.'

Ten minutes.

And now the stage manager calls for silence. He has a small book in his hand from which he is reading aloud. 'Are all the props in place? Yes. Is everybody in costume?

Yes. Made up? Yes. Are the personal props with the right person? Yes. Are those persons relaxed? Er ... yes. Been to the toilet? Hey, you all been to the loo?'

What a question. It would take me an hour to be unpicked and sewn up again, by which time the play would be over.

'Reveal yourself and flee.' Another gulp.

'Reveal yourself and fleeee.'

Five minutes.

Now everyone is smiling nervously and wishing everyone else to break a leg and Foxy is flexing his curtain-pulling muscles.

One minute

Everybody is taking their places. And I have the most unpleasant feeling that I might want to go to the loo.

A hush falls.

The audience is silent.

Expectant.

Foxy's hands are hard upon the yellow cord.

The stage manager calls, 'House lights down. Stage lights up.'

The curtains slide back to reveal a breathtakingly beautiful set, brilliantly lit with multicoloured lights and spotlights.

When Weasel jingles onto centre stage and we hear, '"My mood is sombre, quiet and reflective,"' we know that *this is it*!

And I also know that whereas a short time ago I thought I might want to go to the loo, now it's definite. (*Reveal, reveal, reveal.*)

I try to sit down. I can't.

To pace or not to pace? I will pace.

No, I can't pace. The only place to pace is by the loo.

'*Ahhhh!*'

'*Aawwwwwwwwwwwwwwwwwwwwwwww!*'

'*Uuuuuuuuuuuuuuuuuuuuuuuuuuuuuuuuuuuuuuuuu!*'

Chook and his team are sighing most beautifully which means that the Lady Imogen, with her hand to her brow, is flowing confidently away.

I breathe deeply: 1-2-3-4. 1-2-3-4.

'"Lower the drawbridge!"' roars Mario, every inch a bad king.

This is followed by a long collective sigh. Not from the audience, but from everybody backstage as the drawbridge slides down. And stays there.

I am starting to feel pain.

Sir is looking more confident. Everybody is looking more confident. Everything is going extremely well indeed. (*Reveal, reveal, reveal.*)

With a final blood-curdling howl, the bad king is dead for a ducat, dead, and is theatrically heaved out from behind the beautiful spy screen.

I need to go badly. I need to go desperately.

The Brain can be heard declaring, without the slightest hint of a hiccup, '"Never fear, my dearest, I will not rest until we are united forever in our rightful realm."'

This is followed by silence as he sits on the gold-encrusted throne. And since everybody remains silent we assume (unless they have all gone to sleep) that the throne holds together.

I need to go desperately. Desperately!

I do bending exercises, little half bends because of the stiffness of my chain mail. That's better. Bend up ... bend down ...

From the stage comes, '"Did I hear the sound of hooves?"' and the nice resonance of coconut shells clip-clopping away.

Oh, I am bursting!

Then the sound of the bad knights storming the castle.

I've never been in such pain.

Now the voice of Weasel declares, '"The one whom you seek is amongst us."'

There is another collective sigh of relief as the portcullis swings up and the bad knights charge across it, accompanied by harmonic *clip-clopping*.

I'm gonna burst.

I dig my fingers into my chain mail. I sink my teeth into my lips. I draw blood.

The time limps by.

I am in agony.

Pace, bend, pace, bend, pace, pinch. Pinch, dig ... breathe deeply ...

Around me I see happy, cooperative faces as knights and ladies and kings both good and bad come and go. Everybody is smelling the sweet smell of success and anticipating the final roar of applause.

'*Erg!*'

'*Uuuuuuuuuuuuuuu!*'

'*Eeee rrr gggg!*'

'*Uuuuuuuuuuuuuuuuuuuuuuuuuuuuu!*'

'*Ahhhh aaaahhhhhh aaaaaahhhhhhhhhhhhhhhhhhhhhhhhh!*'
'*Erggggg!*'
'*Egggg!*'
'*Uuuuuuuuuuuuuuuuuuuuuuuuuuuuuuuuuuuuuuuuuuuuuuuuuuuu!*'

Now the good knight says to the bad knight, '"I have you in my power. You cannot escape,"' which means we're up to the sword fight where the bad knight breathes his last.

'*Ohhhhhh . . .*'

Think. Think of something sad. Take your mind off yourself. Think. Think of rattlesnakes. Think of rattlesnakes curled up on a rock. On a very large rock. Think of rattlesnakes twisting, turning, coiling through thick grass to a water hole. No! No! Think of something else. Quick! Grandma. Grandma's ears. Think of Grandma's ears. Two ears, one two, one two, one two . . . Think of Myrtle. Myrtle's bowels. Bowels, bottoms, loos . . . No! NO! Think of . . . think of—

'You're on!'

'What?'

'Coming up to your cue.'

It's here. I can hear it.

'"The moment, at last, is come."'

That's my cue.

And I'm on.

I'm treading the boards and breathing heavily and digging my fingers into my chain mail. All eyes are upon me.

I stare into the black, gaping void. And I go blank.

There's something I've got to say. I've got to say a line. The whole play hinges on it.

But no. I speak. I open my mouth and with vocal projection that would shatter bricks, I bellow:

‘“*Reveal yourself and pee!*”’

Ring Down the Curtain

The play is over. The curtains are closing to thunderous applause.

I shoot to the loo.

'Everyone on stage!' Sir bawls.

We line up in our places. The curtains open again, then close again, and open and close, and open and close like in a professional theatre.

And they're still clapping. The daggy moronic thing has worked.

We have made it work.

We're all punching each other and slapping each other on the back and grinning from ear to ear. We're laughing and shouting. And Sir is laughing and shouting louder than anyone.

And it's all because of my line.

When I realised what I'd said I thought I would die on the spot of mortification and humiliation. (Plus bladder failure.)

There was dead silence.

Then there was a tiny titter. Followed by another titter or two, followed by a couple of little giggles. Then suddenly there was a great big belly guffaw and the whole place exploded into laughter.

And then I heard something familiar. It was a particular laugh. My mother's laugh. Then I heard something else that was familiar. And again it was a laugh. My father's laugh.

And then I heard something most unfamiliar. In fact I can't remember when I last heard it. It was the two of them laughing together.

Now that the play is over, people are clambering up onto the stage and they're telling me that my line was the best thing about the whole production. Because by the time it was delivered, most of the audience was asleep.

I haven't seen my family yet. I start searching for them in the crowd.

There they are, Mum, Dad and Grandma with their arms around each other, pushing their way towards me. And still laughing.

I laugh. They laugh. Grandma laughs. Grandma's friend, Ida, laughs and Myrtle laughs.

And Bugs is saying that since I am bound for stardom, I'll need to study the great Shakespearian masterpieces that are available on DVD—which means getting a television set, like next week.

And Mum looks at Dad and Dad looks at Mum and they both look at me. And it's the look of love. You know it, because you can't disguise it. It's just there.

Suddenly there's a burst of music from the sound system. Someone has turned the volume up to max. And now people are pushing back the seats and stacking them against the walls and the place has turned into a disco.

Everyone's grabbing someone and rock-and-rolling away. It's party time.

The Ape's gone ape on his guitar. Weed's singing to the beat of Chook's rock-and-rolling coconut shells from the top of the drawbridge. Nigel is waltzing this way and that, his spy screen (turned cloak), floating out behind him. The Brain is dubbing me Knight of the Night with his (by this time) severed sword. Jemima's dancing around me and with each whirl, cracks me on the head with her cone-shaped hat (which, as anyone knows, is a sign of appreciation). Jonesey and Weasel are dancing round and about with Angie, Mad-Dog and Mario. Matthew Wigg is trying to dance, too, on his one good leg, and Spin Bowler is joining in with his one good ear. Spud is laughing as he watches Foxy rock-and-roll with Mrs Amelia Throsby, who is doing a great deal of happy but heavy breathing from the diaphragm.

Weed makes a very well-executed leap from the draw-bridge and takes Grandma off rock-and-rolling down the hall. And Bugs is leaping too, trying to keep up with the black-stockinged legs of Miss Joan Effington-Smythe.

Sir is trying to make a speech. Everyone's too busy singing and dancing to listen. So Sir gives up and joins in.

Mrs Babbage, the principal, has a go at giving a speech, but since nobody can hear her either, she grabs the deputy principal by the coat-tails and off they go, too, rock-and-rolling away. And what am I doing during all this very excellent activity?

Well, I'll tell you.

I'm rock-and-rolling, too. With Lizzie.

And I'll tell you another thing. Her eyes are the bluest I've ever seen.

So there you have it!